PUNCH
LIKE A GIRL

PUNCH
LIKE A GIRL

KAREN KROSSING

ORCA BOOK PUBLISHERS

Library and Archives Canada Cataloguing in Publication

Krossing, Karen, 1965–, author
Punch like a girl / Karen Krossing.

Issued in print and electronic formats.
ISBN 978-1-4598-0828-7 (pbk.).—ISBN 978-1-4598-0829-4 (pdf).—
ISBN 978-1-4598-0830-0 (epub)

I. Title.
PS8571.R776P85 2015   jc813'.6   C2014-906681-3
C2014-906682-1

First published in the United States, 2015
Library of Congress Control Number: 2014952065

Summary: After Tori is sexually assaulted, she tells no one and her rage and confusion erupt
into violent behavior that mystifies her friends and family.

*Orca Book Publishers is dedicated to preserving the environment and
has printed this book on Forest Stewardship Council® certified paper.*

Orca Book Publishers gratefully acknowledges the support for its publishing programs
provided by the following agencies: the Government of Canada through the Canada Book
Fund and the Canada Council for the Arts, and the Province of British Columbia
through the BC Arts Council and the Book Publishing Tax Credit.

Cover design by Chantal Gabriell
Cover image by Shutterstock and iStockphoto
Author photo by Owen Captures (owencaptures.com)

ORCA BOOK PUBLISHERS   ORCA BOOK PUBLISHERS
PO Box 5626, STN. B   PO Box 468
VICTORIA, BC CANADA   CUSTER, WA USA
V8R 6S4   98240-0468

www.orcabook.com
Printed and bound in Canada.

18 17 16 15 • 4 3 2 1

For my girls

SHEAR

to cut away

I wake in the dark, breathing hard, my hair tangled across my face, strands caught in my mouth. Not even sleep can slow the constant pounding in my head.

My eyes water. My nose runs. I kick against the sheets wrapped tightly around my legs. As I sweep the hair off my face, I fight the urge to retch.

When my stomach settles, I stumble across the hallway to the upstairs bathroom. The light from the streetlamp falls across the double sink. I stare into the mirror, repulsed by my hair.

It has to go.

First, I tie off two ponytails, each more than eight inches long. Next, I cut close to the scalp with Mom's haircutting shears and lay two hunks of curly, blond hair across the back of the toilet.

The girl in the mirror still has too much hair.

I hack at the tufts with Dad's electric clippers. Why can I still feel Matt's fingers stroking my hair, praising it? *It's your best feature,* he used to say.

Sobs rattle my chest. When the clippers become too dull to cut, I toss them in the sink, cracking their plastic casing.

Dad will be pissed, but I don't care. I empty the drawers until I find his straight razor and shaving soap.

I cry out when the razor slices my skin just above my right ear. Blood trickles down my neck. A stain spreads slowly across my lacy, white pajama top.

When my head is shaved raw, I stop.

A tough girl glares back at me from the mirror.

GNAW

≷ *to wear down* ≷

The next day, I let Alena run her hand over my freshly shaved head.

"Geez, Tori." She bumps into a display of spring sandals. "It's smooth, like satin."

It's Monday after school, and we're strolling through Glencrest Mall, heading for the post-office counter inside the drugstore. I'm wearing low-rise skinny jeans with a yellow H&M sweater and ballet flats. A typical outfit for me, but it feels off, like it doesn't suit me anymore.

"And you're just going to mail your hair to some company?" Jamarlo touches his stumpy dreads protectively.

"Yup." I hoist the oversized envelope under my arm. "They make wigs for kids who've gone bald, so I couldn't resist," I say for the hundredth time today.

"Kids with cancer—how sad." Alena fingers her own hair as if she's ready to cut it off and hand it over. Her dark Mediterranean waves are forcibly straightened each morning. "But won't you miss your hair? It was a guy magnet."

"So what?" I say. "Those kids are facing worse than I am."

Jamarlo raises his eyebrows. Alena glances at me.

"I mean, I'm healthy, and I live in a suburb where nothing bad is supposed to happen, in a house where the fridge is always full." My voice catches. "Life is great for people like us. That's why we have to give back."

Alena squeezes my arm in that concerned way she has. "I get that you've got a big heart, but does the head shaving have anything to do with Matt? He was crazy about your hair, but you didn't need to shave it to chase him away."

"Yeah, the knee to the groin was clear enough." Jamarlo winces.

"Matt has been erased from my memory banks." I ignore the pressure building inside my head. How can I talk about what happened when even thinking about it makes me sick? "I'm off the market until the guys our age are mature enough to date," I say.

Alena snorts. "Maybe in ten years, if you're lucky."

Jamarlo shoots us a pissed-off look. "We're not all jerks."

"Of course, you're the one exception." I drape an arm over his shoulder. He's only a bit bigger than me, which isn't saying much, since I'm five feet tall and I weigh ninety-nine pounds after a plate of spaghetti.

"Damn right I am." Jamarlo nods, still frowning.

"What exactly did Matt do at Carmen's party on Saturday night?" Alena asks as we turn into the drugstore. "You haven't said. I mean, he showed up with Melody, but you'd broken up with him a week before, so—"

"We argued. I kneed him. It's over." I force my voice to stay steady, tenderly prodding the razor cut above my ear.

"But—" Alena begins.

"You know, it isn't easy to get rid of hair. In the end, I had to use my dad's straight razor." I blabber on, not mentioning how freaked out my parents were when they saw my head at breakfast. How Mom almost spilled her coffee down her blouse, and Dad choked on his toast. "Did you know that women who were accused of sleeping with German soldiers during the second World War were forcibly shaved in Paris after the war? Mr. Hadley told us about it in World History."

"Brutal," Jamarlo says.

Alena wrinkles her nose. At least she's stopped asking questions.

We don't have to wait long at the post-office counter. When the clerk gives my head a hostile look, I practice

5

my new don't-mess-with-me stare on her. I guess my fake-polite face disappeared with my hair. Then I watch the clerk place my package in the outgoing bin; suddenly I'm desperate to be rid of it.

As we wander out of the drugstore, I'm dizzy. We pass a café with giggling girls at one of the tables. When scrawny Jamarlo struts for them, the girls whisper and turn away. It's rough—Jamarlo is friends with a lot of girls, but no one wants to date him.

"Bald can be sexy," he says once we pass the girls. "Except for Britney Spears during her cosmic meltdown. I'd give her a two out of ten on the female bald-o-meter."

"Sexy is overrated," I say.

"Since when are you against sexy?" Jamarlo pretends to pole-dance using me as the pole.

I push him away, but nicely. "Since sexy started to suck."

"Uh-oh. Someone's got the break-up blues," Jamarlo teases.

"Wouldn't you if you'd just ditched a jerk?"

"You know, Tori"—Alena keeps her tone light, as if she knows I'm tensing up—"your new look makes your eyes bigger and your neck longer. You're just lucky you have a nicely shaped head. You could've had lumps under all that gorgeous hair."

"Or pus-filled scars." Jamarlo grins.

"Your face is a pus-filled scar, Jamarlo." I pretend to punch him.

He pretends to duck, as always.

The familiar routine calms me a bit.

"Oh, look." Alena points to Felipe's Glam Boutique. "We have to check out the dresses in the sale section. Do you mind, Jamarlo?"

"'Course not." He flips up the collar of his purple plaid shirt and sets his black-brimmed hat low on his forehead. "I'm cool with it."

"Hey, Tori, we've got our own pimp!" Alena laughs.

A middle-aged woman in a pastel suit frowns at Alena, but I scowl until she looks away. Is everyone in the mall a jerk today?

We pass the glittery, low-cut dresses in the window and head into Felipe's—the most exciting shop in this suburban paradise.

Inside, Felipe—the flamboyant, silver-haired owner—is showing versions of the little black dress to a twenty-something woman and her boyfriend, who has a serious Neanderthal forehead. The boyfriend wraps a protective arm around his girl's waist and narrows his eyes as he watches Felipe swing dresses off a rack with a flourish and display them across his hairy forearm.

"Did you hear about the anti-prom?" Alena's brown eyes sparkle in the overhead lights.

"Not really." I frown. The last thing I want is to go to another party.

"Well, we have to go! It's June 23 at some club. It'll be way more fun than the official prom—better music, no teachers." Alena tugs us toward the sale section at the back of the store, near the dressing rooms and the three-way mirror. "I hear they're hiring a DJ and everything."

"And it's only for grade elevens," Jamarlo adds. "Because we're not too lame to enjoy it."

"We'll need to find dresses for it." Alena runs her hands over the rainbow of dresses in the sale section. She holds up a full-length turquoise gown with a Marilyn Monroe-style halter top and ruffles from the hips down. "What do you think of this one for you?"

"The party's seven weeks away." I try not to roll my eyes, even though a few weeks ago I would've loved any dress from Felipe's. "And won't it be casual? No one will be wearing a dress like that."

"What's wrong with it?" Alena twirls, letting the skirt flare. "I'd wear it. It's drop-dead gorgeous."

"Anti-proms are supposed to be subversive, Alena. That dress is too"—I notice the hurt expression on her face and back off—"traditional."

Jamarlo snorts.

Alena sticks her tongue out at me. "Nothing is more subversive than showing up at an anti-prom in formal wear."

She holds the dress in place and examines her reflection in the three-way mirror. "What are you going to wear? Jeans?"

I flash back to Carmen Carter's house party: Matt finding me on the makeshift dance floor to grind against my jeans, zipper to zipper. *"You owe me, Tori. I've waited long enough."* His arms snaking around me, forcing me closer. Me yanking free. Melody shooting me deadly looks from across the crowded room.

"I'm not going." I lean against a row of dresses and crush the crisp fabric of a honey-colored taffeta dress.

"What?" Alena almost drops the gown. "Tori, you have to!"

I pretend to examine the dresses. I hate to disappoint her, but I just can't go.

"Come on, Tori. You can be my date." Jamarlo slips his arms around my waist.

"Who will wear the dress?" I tease, plastering on a smile. Then I grip his hand and lead him in a fake waltz, sideswiping dresses.

"You'd look great in a tux." Jamarlo laughs.

Alena is still pouting.

"You'd look amazing in this, Jamarlo." I grab a red strapless with a short poufy skirt off a sale rack and hold it up to him, trying to make Alena laugh.

"It's divine." Jamarlo grins as he takes the dress from me. It's actually nice against his brown skin. He links

arms with Alena. "Come on, girlfriend. Let's try these beauties on."

I laugh a little too loudly. Alena sighs.

"Fricking faggot," someone says.

We spin around. It's Neanderthal with his girl, who's clutching a black dress. Neanderthal glares at Jamarlo, his muscled arms crossed.

"What did you say?" Jamarlo grips the red strapless, his face flushing.

I step toward Neanderthal, even though he's twice my size.

"I'm sorry"—I pretend to address Felipe, who's yakking with a preteen and her mother near the cash— "but do you let homophobes shop here?" Felipe may be gay, and I know Jamarlo isn't, but that's not the point.

"Uh, Tori?" Alena slinks into the next row of dresses.

Neanderthal's girl blinks at us with wide, startled eyes.

"Tori, leave it." Jamarlo tugs my arm.

"What'd you call me?" Neanderthal's face gets redder.

Adrenaline pumps through me. The pressure in my head swells. "Was that too big a word for you? How about *stupid*? Do you know what that means?"

"Cut it out, Tori." Jamarlo's voice is a warning.

"No, Jamarlo. He can't call you a—"

"A faggot?" Neanderthal's lip curls. "You need a girl to defend you, faggot?" He makes two meaty fists.

Jamarlo's face goes burgundy.

"So what if he does?" I get into protective position—hands clenched in front of me, ready to defend. My knees tremble.

Neanderthal smirks at my undersized fists. "I bet you punch like a girl."

"You bet I do." I reach up and land a hammerfist on his nose, just like I should have done with Matt.

Alena gasps. Neanderthal's girlfriend shrieks.

"What the hell?" Jamarlo yells.

Neanderthal howls. He ignores the blood oozing from his left nostril and reaches for me.

Terror clogs my veins. I kick him hard in the shin with one of my ballet flats. Once. Twice. Three times.

He moans and clutches his leg, hopping on one foot until he loses his balance, taking out a rack of dresses as he falls.

BEAT

to get seriously pummeled

Half an hour later, we're crammed into a mall-security office that smells like body odor.

My friends are pressed into a corner near the doorway, unable to leave because they're witnesses. I've been forced to sit in a hard-backed chair wedged between a desk and the far wall. One guard stands over me, and another sits behind the desk. When I try to get up, the standing guard puts a hand on my shoulder and pushes me back down.

"Don't touch me!" I'm a quivering mess.

"Sit down!" he barks.

"I said call the cops now!" Neanderthal paces in front of the desk.

Then both my parents rush into the room, still in their work clothes. Mom gets to me first, petting my head as if smoothing my nonexistent hair.

"What's up with you, Tori?" Her tone is curt. "You don't get into fights."

"She does now," Jamarlo mutters.

Alena elbows him, frowning.

"Did anyone hurt you?" Dad's upper lip twitches as he eyes Neanderthal.

"I'm fine," I say, even though I'm not.

The weary guard behind the desk explains to my parents about my supposedly "unprovoked" assault on Neanderthal.

"He started it," I tell my parents. "He insulted Jamarlo, and he was coming after me too."

Jamarlo eyes the exit like he's ready to bolt. Dad's chest puffs out like he's had pec-enhancement surgery. Mom puts on her uptight face, which can only mean she's going to get her way or rationally argue someone to death, whichever comes first.

"Call the cops already," Neanderthal says to the desk guard.

"Of course we can call the police…" The guard shuffles papers. Maybe he wants to avoid paperwork. "Or we can figure out a solution."

"An excellent idea," Mom says.

"I want her arrested!" Neanderthal glares across the desk.

Neanderthal's girl stands at his side. When she holds a plastic bag of ice to his swollen nose, he whacks her hand in a way that reminds me of Matt. I fight the urge to vomit.

The desk guard reluctantly reaches for his cordless phone.

"No, wait, please!" Dad calls out. "My little girl wouldn't hurt anyone. This is a mistake."

The desk guard pauses. Maybe it's because Dad's wearing his mail-carrier outfit. Maybe the guard feels a kinship with another man in a uniform.

Neanderthal squares off against Dad. They're the same height, but Dad's twice as old. "Are you calling me a liar, old man?" A drop of ice water slides down his ugly nose and dilutes the blood congealed above his lip.

"She's only seventeen and half your size." Dad pokes a finger into Neanderthal's beefy chest. "How could she break your nose?"

"Geez, Dad!" I leap up and get forced down again. "They showed us how in the self-defense classes you made me take."

Dad's neck muscles tighten, and I know he's remembering his rant when I was in grade eight and developing boobs. *Any girl of mine needs to learn how to protect herself*, he'd said.

Alena, who witnessed the rant, gives a vigorous nod. She came to self-defense classes with me, although she was always afraid to throw a punch.

"Everyone calm down," Mom orders, wedging herself between Dad and Neanderthal. "I'm sure we can work something out."

"Work it out with the cops." Neanderthal grinds his teeth at Dad, who's glaring over Mom's shoulder at him. "Make the damn call now, or I will," he tells the desk guard without taking his eyes off Dad.

The desk guard sighs and reaches for the phone.

Dad grabs it first. "No one's making any calls," he says. His face is flushed, and his look practically dares Neanderthal to come at him.

"Enough theatrics," Mom snaps. She slides one hand around Dad, pries the phone from his grip and passes it to the desk guard, her lips pressed into a firm line. "Call the police, if you must. Although we could talk out a solution in a *civilized* manner."

Dad glares at Mom. She ignores him. How did I end up in this mess?

"That would save me some paperwork." The desk guard grips the phone defensively.

"Of course it would." Mom smiles at the guard and then faces Neanderthal. "I realize that we got off on the wrong foot here, Mr. Rayfield. I can see you're a respectable young man."

Not the approach I'd take. Dad scowls. Neanderthal's eyes narrow, but he wipes at the blood above his lip as if he has a sudden urge to be respectable.

"I wonder if you'd listen to a proposal." Mom glances at the desk guard, who nods as if to say, *Keep going, lady.*

Neanderthal's in for it now. A "proposal" is one of my mother's tactics to get what she wants.

"Why should I?" Neanderthal grunts.

"Please, hear me out. I acknowledge that Tori's behavior was out of line, no matter what you did or didn't do to provoke her." My mother's a middle-school teacher, and she knows when to pull out the teacher talk.

Neanderthal nods dumbly.

"And there should be a consequence for such behavior, maybe something like"—she pauses—"community service?"

Neanderthal scowls. "What good will that do?"

"It'll teach Tori that punching you was going too far." She glances critically at me.

I look away.

Neanderthal tilts his head to one side, examining me.

I resist the urge to point out that Neanderthal started it all, so why am I the only one to be punished?

"You mean like working in an old folks' home or something?" Neanderthal's girl asks. "She could work at that place where your grandfather—"

"I don't want her near him." Neanderthal scowls again, like I'm the dangerous one.

"We can work out an informal arrangement," Mom says. "We don't need to get the police involved. After all, they may question how such a small girl could hurt such a large man."

Neanderthal's eyebrows rise. I want to point out that size has nothing to do with throwing a good punch, but I bite my tongue.

"Even if we call the police, and they do arrest her," Mom continues, "it'll likely never go to trial. So if you and I work out a solution here, we can control the terms." She goes on about how community service would teach me to face the consequences of my actions. "My husband and I would personally oversee her community-service hours and make sure they're completed."

"You expect me to believe that? I'm not stupid, you know," Neanderthal says, although the thick eyebrows, dull eyes and half-open mouth suggest otherwise.

"Of course you aren't." Mom keeps a straight face. "But if you agree to community service, you have my personal assurance that she'll complete it. I'll even provide you with proof—maybe with signed time sheets from wherever she volunteers? And you won't need to waste your time at a court hearing. It's a win-win. Shall we say a hundred hours?"

Neanderthal stares down my mother. "That's nothing," he says. "Double it."

As if he could do the math. But I don't care what the number is. If my parents are overseeing it, there's no way I'll have to do community service for an act of self-defense. I mean, maybe I shouldn't have hit him, but Neanderthal is a complete homophobe and a bully.

When the deal is done, I'm finally sprung from the security office. Mom and Neanderthal settled on 175 hours of community service, to be monitored by my parents. Even though I hated being talked about like a dog that's getting punished for drinking the toilet water, I'm grateful Mom's tactics kept the police at bay.

"We should call the cops on him," I say to Mom once we finally part ways with Neanderthal and his girl.

We head toward the closest mall exit.

"That guy was a jerk." Alena looks suitably offended.

Jamarlo frowns down at his high-tops.

Dad trails two steps behind, glancing back at Neanderthal. I'm sure he'd love to go at him, and I'd bet on Dad to win even though he's older and has a bit of a paunch. Dad used to be a bouncer, so he knows how to fight.

Mom purses her lips. "You're lucky you got out of it with just community service."

"That was a brilliant idea, Mom. I won't have to do it if you're monitoring it."

"You most certainly will." She stops to stare at me. "Down to the last minute."

My friends glance at each other.

"What?" Why is she turning on me?

"I didn't want to get into this in front of your friends, Tori, but your dad and I are more than a little worried about you. First you shave your head in the middle of the night, and now this? I can protect you from police charges, but I can't let you get away with punching a stranger at the mall. What were you thinking?"

Alena studies the floor tiles. Jamarlo looks grim.

I feel like I've been punched by my own mother. "But he—"

"Don't make excuses for your behavior." Mom frowns. "Maybe community service will help you realize the consequences of your actions. As for why you're acting so strangely…well, we can have a long chat about that at home."

God, no. My face heats up. I need some serious Alena-and-Jamarlo time to help me through this injustice. I grab my friends' arms and pull them with me to walk way ahead of my parents.

"Victoria." Mom's voice is stern. "I'm only doing this because I care. You'll understand when you're a parent."

As if. I ignore her, even though she keeps pace behind us.

"That was insane," Alena says. "And now you need to do community service? Even though you were in his face, what about him?"

"I wasn't in his face," I say. "I was protecting us from an asshole."

"Of course." Alena glances at Jamarlo like he might explain. "Listen, I know the break-up with Matt rattled you, so if you ever want to talk…"

Why does everyone want to talk? I frown at Alena and then weave my fingers into Jamarlo's.

"Hey, Jamarlo, were you actually going to try on that dress?" I smile. "Because it would have suited you."

"Tori—" Alena begins.

"Alena, there's nothing to talk about," I say, trying to keep the edge out of my voice. "Really."

Jamarlo pulls away from me. "What's wrong with you?" His eyes are dark. "Why did you leap in front of me? I could have handled that guy!"

I stare, confused. "I didn't mean—"

"It doesn't matter what you meant, Tori. It's what you did. You mouth off for me, but I can take care of myself."

"I know that!"

"Then why didn't you stop when I told you to?"

"I was trying to help." My jaw clenches.

"Help me look like a wimp?" He spins away, hands in the air.

"Jamarlo," Alena says, "give her a break. She's been through a lot—"

"Yeah? So have I. In case you didn't notice, Tori just made me look like a wuss!"

"But Jamarlo—"

"Forget it, Tori." He walks away. "Just do me a favor. Get it together before you hurt someone else."

Another punch. My gut aches. My own people are beating me when I'm down?

"Jamarlo, wait," Alena calls. But he keeps going.

I want to run after him, crack a joke so we can laugh it off, tell him it was all a mistake. But the pressure in my head increases again, and I feel the weight of my mother's hawkish stare, her talons ready to snatch me up and whisk me home for an endless lecture.

I march to the exit before she can make another scene.

BURNED

to be exposed to heat long enough to force a change

O n Tuesday evening, I slip into the kitchen from the carport, where I parked Dad's Civic. My sweat from soccer practice has cooled, leaving my skin clammy. With Alena smoking hot in goal and me a wall of defense, we're ready for our first game of the season.

I dump my bag in the corner by the cappuccino maker and inhale the scent of pepperoni. At the table, Joel, my annoying dork of a brother, and his friend Roger are gulping down the remains of two double-cheese, meatloaded pizzas. Roger sits like a lump in front of his plate while Joel leans his pointy elbows on the table. I can hear Mom and Dad talking in the living room, settled in for their end-of-day chat. If I'm lucky, I can avoid the conversation about community service that's been on repeat since yesterday—as well as any comments about my shaved head.

After I shaved, I had to endure a barrage of questions from my parents: "*Why did you shave it?*" "*For charity.*" "*In the middle of the night?*" "*I couldn't sleep, so I shaved my head. What's the big deal?*"

Since the mall, the questions have gotten more intense: "*Why did you feel the need to punch that man?*" "*Come on. You know he was a jerk.*" "*Didn't we teach you to handle conflict in other ways?*" "*You did, Mom, but Dad's been known to throw a punch in his time, and no one made him do community service.*"

Leaving my cleats on, I pull out a chair across from Joel and Roger and snatch a slice before they're all gone. I sink my teeth into the cheesy goodness as my butt hits the chair—eating food is the only way to claim it when Joel and Roger are around.

"Hey, younger sibling." Joel kicks me under the table.

I'm still wearing my shin pads, so I ignore him. Pestering me until I flip out is one of Joel's favorite pastimes—a pleasure I try to deny him as much as possible.

"How's it going?" I ask Roger with my mouth full.

Roger nods and chews. "Nice hair," he grunts. It's not a come-on—more of an observation.

"Thanks."

"That's not what the parental units said," Joel says to Roger. He grins, taking a swipe at my head, but I lean my chair back, balancing on the two rear legs—one of my standard defensive moves.

Joel is sixteen months older than me and only one grade ahead in school. He should be finishing high school in June, but he's not that motivated, even though he's brilliant in math and science. Instead, he prefers to play practical jokes on his teachers, flirt with the grade-eleven girls who fawn over him—a disgusting spectacle—and challenge Roger to burping contests in the cafeteria.

"Tori tried to get arrested yesterday," Joel says. "It was pretty messed up."

"Shut up, Joel," I say between bites. I don't need to listen to crap from him as well.

"Really? What happened?"

"Nothing." I give Joel a change-the-subject-or-face-your-doom look.

"She punched some jerk at the mall." Joel snorts when he laughs. "I wish I could have been there. Apparently, he was six feet tall and built. Tori took him out with one punch."

"Impressive." Roger stuffs in more pizza.

"And stupid," Joel adds.

"You would know stupid, Joel," I say. Not that I need Roger's approval, but I don't mind having someone on my side for a change.

"What I don't get is why you got so pissed off." Joel smirks. "Hey, maybe Mom could sign you up for some anger-management classes. I wonder if she's thought of that yet."

I silently count to ten, determined not to let him get to me.

When I grab a second slice of pizza, Roger freezes in mid-chomp to stare at the final piece, sitting alone in one of the boxes. He glances at Joel, who sizes him up.

They trade maniacal smiles.

I take a massive bite, gripping my slice tighter. Anyone who believes in the possibility of world peace hasn't seen my brother and his friend fight for the last of the pizza.

When Roger reaches for it, Joel slaps his hand away, and the battle begins. Soon they're knocking over kitchen chairs and wrestling on the floor, grunting and laughing. It's like having an Ultimate Fighting match in our kitchen.

"Cut it out," I say when they bump against my chair. I used to wrestle with my brother, but I've matured.

When Mom and Dad arrive in the kitchen, I'm hoping they'll be too distracted by Joel and Roger to lecture me. Dad hauls Joel off Roger, grunting with the effort. Joel, lean and lanky, lands a last punch. Roger, round and gelatinous, lumbers to his feet.

"What have we told you about fighting in the kitchen?" The tone of Mom's voice makes them blink and glance around at the scattered chairs and pizza boxes on the floor. "You could've hurt each other!"

"Or broken something." Dad gives Joel a slight shake before releasing him.

"Sorry 'bout that." Roger rights a chair.

"Me too." Joel grabs the last slice of pizza, which has fallen upside down on the floor, and shoves half of it into his mouth. Nice.

"I expect both you boys to clean up. And if we catch you fighting again…" Mom targets them with her full-on teacher glare until the air between them sizzles.

Roger shrinks. Joel nods dutifully, still chewing.

Mom turns on her heel, letting her threat hang. "Tori," she calls on the way out, her voice ominous, "come into the living room when you're done. We need to chat."

Not again.

"A little roughhousing is one thing, but this is too much," Dad says to Joel, gesturing at the pizza boxes, the toppled chairs and the kitchen in general. "You should be grateful for what we give you. I didn't have nearly as much as you when I was a kid." He trails Mom into the living room.

My ungrateful brother smirks at me like he's enjoying that I'm about to be railed. "*Hasta la vista*, baby," he says in his Terminator voice, his mouth still full.

I take as long as I can to remove my cleats, socks and shin pads. When I hope Mom has forgotten about me,

I breeze through the living room, aiming for the stairs to the second floor.

"Where are you going?" Dad asks.

"I've just got to change out of these clothes." And take a shower, check my messages, do my homework and go to bed without any conversations about shaving or community service.

"Not so fast." Mom pats the couch beside her. "Sit down."

I trudge back. Mom's at one end of the couch, and Dad's at the other. I perch on the arm of a leather recliner near Dad.

"I still can't get used to that haircut." Mom shakes her head, eyeing me. "I know you wanted to donate you hair, but I still don't understand what possessed you to shave it all off."

I shrug. "Like Dad said, it's just a phase. Don't worry about it."

"It makes you look…" She pauses.

"Tough," Dad finishes, sounding a little proud.

"I guess it does."

"Yes, well…" Mom frowns. "We wanted to talk because we found you a community-service job." She holds out a flyer. The headline reads *You Can Help*. There's a photo of a scrawny cat.

I cringe.

"The humane society would be a good place to do your hours. We know you like animals."

I picture cleaning out poop from hundreds of cages while imprisoned dogs and cats stare at me with gloomy eyes. "Not when they're waiting to be put down." I can imagine staging a massive rescue of the caged animals. "I don't even get why I need to do any—"

"Don't start that again," Dad says. "Your mother promised you'd do community service, and you're going to do it."

Great. Now he's onside with Mom. I hate when they get along.

"But it's not fair." I raise my voice. "Why should I be the only one punished? Neanderthal started it."

"Neanderthal? Mr. Rayfield has a name, Tori." Mom gives me a disapproving look.

"Who cares what his—"

"You may not agree with his opinions," Mom interrupts, "but he didn't hit anyone. You did. Really, Tori, we're struggling to understand what's going on with you. Help us out here."

"But he was talking crap about Jamarlo. Why can't you—?"

"And that was a good reason to break Mr. Rayfield's nose? You could have notified the manager, called 9-1-1, left the store. There were so many other choices."

"You might have been hurt." Dad stands and paces, his eyebrows knotted. "You should be more careful."

"Like you, Dad? I could tell you wanted to go at him."

"But he didn't," Mom says. "Tori, you can choose a place to do community service by the end of this week, or we will. Either way, you're going to do your 175 hours. It's for your own good."

"But Mom—"

"Listen to your mother." Dad's voice is firm.

I take one look at their faces and swallow my words. What's the point in arguing when they can't hear me? Life is full of injustices. This is one battle I'm going to lose.

$\sim_\mathfrak{G}$

At school the next day, I browse places to do community service, since I don't want my parents lurking over my shoulder. Ms. Mink, the guidance counselor with the gaudy jewelry and excessive perfume, keeps a list of volunteer jobs; she's always keen to "get students involved."

After I escape Ms. Mink's nosy questions about how I'm doing in my classes, I sit at the bank of computers in front of the floor-to-ceiling windows that look into the hall. I'm distracted by the people wandering past with boxes of fries from the cafeteria or cold drinks from the 7-Eleven in the strip mall across the street.

The grid of wires embedded in the guidance-office windows makes me feel imprisoned, like I can't be trusted beyond these walls.

I watch Joel saunter past, acting the goof, as usual. He drops ice from his drink down the front of a girl's shirt. Roger laughs like an oversized buffoon while the girl shrieks and swats at Joel, flirting madly. Another guy walks by with a swagger, just like Matt does. It's not him, since Matt goes to the Catholic school with Melody, but the sight of that swagger knocks the air out of my lungs.

I'm sucking in a breath, wishing I'd never met Matt, when I see Jamarlo with Alena. Jamarlo is gesturing wildly and grinning in a way that makes me miss him like crazy. He's probably telling a hilarious story about what happened in class; he can make anything funny. I sigh and look down at the computer screen.

I surf the websites of a few places to volunteer at. No way am I joining a decorating team for a health and beauty fair—I'll never make flowers out of Kleenex. A job as a retail worker at a health center isn't helping anyone out, other than saving the center from paying decent wages. And I can't be a pet-therapy volunteer since I don't have a pet to bring, although I briefly consider Joel for the role.

I scratch at the prickly stubble on my head; it's getting itchy as the hair grows in. At least my shaved head is attracting fewer stares at school. The gossip queens have found better targets.

Then I find a volunteer posting that doesn't look too bad:

CHILD AND YOUTH VOLUNTEER

Haven Women's Shelter is looking for a volunteer to assist our child and youth workers with after-school and evening programs for children. The shelter supports and houses women and their children fleeing violence. This volunteer will provide support to the children living in the shelter and act as a positive role model.

I lean back in my chair and stare at the screen. *Children fleeing violence.* Those kids would want my help—not like Jamarlo. Maybe I could even teach them a thing or two about standing up for themselves.

I submit an application online and then head to class. Since I have to do community service, I'd rather it be at Haven.

KiCK

to use your foot as a weapon

O n Friday night, I'm hoofing a soccer ball at Alena, who's warming up in net.

The sun is low in the sky behind her, and her long shadow falls over me. When she drop-kicks the ball back to me, I hoof it again, aiming for the top-left corner. Alena jumps, smacking the ball out of bounds easily.

"Good one," I call, going after it.

Alena used to be in rep soccer until she got trampled one too many times by aggressive forwards. Now we play house league together, with me as center defense and her in goal. Our team is strong this year, packed with girls who know how to handle a ball and have fun. Tonight the Screamin' Demons—we named ourselves that because of our red shirts—will face the Babes in Blue, a nauseating name. Alena and I renamed them the Blue Bitches, since they somehow stack the Blue team every year with the same eight or so nasty yet gorgeous players.

As I jog toward the ball, my shaved head attracts the usual stares from players as well as the few people gathered on the sidelines. When I spot Matt, pain registers in my chest, and my head throbs. Does he have to be here? Now?

Matt looks like a young Leonardo DiCaprio, only with black hair and a smile that used to knock me horizontal. Right now he's aiming his sickening smile at Melody, who just happens to be a hard-hitting forward on the Blue Bitches. She thrusts her boobs at Matt, tossing her blond ponytail and posing with her Barbie-doll legs.

It figures they would hook up. Did he even wait until we were through?

Matt does a double take at the stubble on my head. My limbs become gawky, and I stumble over my feet. Melody gives me a deadly glare. She probably thinks I want to get back with Matt, but I'm praying he's turned off. I dribble the ball away, trying to act like he doesn't threaten my world.

When I veer back toward Alena, Jamarlo is leaning against the goalpost, chatting with her. As I near, Jamarlo's eyes bore into me and then look away. Alena starts talking faster and waving her arms, like her Greek mother does when she's upset.

"Hey, Jamarlo." I jog over, still shaky, and boot the ball so that it lands at his feet like an offering.

He ignores it, his eyes anywhere but on me. "See you, Alena." He turns toward the sidelines.

"Wait, Jamarlo, just talk to Tori," Alena pleads.

"Why should I?" He turns back, his eyes flaming. "So she can make some lame excuse?"

Alena puts her hands on her hips. "Don't make a big deal of this, Jamarlo. Tori was just upset because of the break-up. Now she's—"

"Just leave it, Alena." I press my lips together. I've been off my game this week, but he's too pissed off to talk, and I hate listening to Alena argue for him to forgive me.

Alena gapes at me. Jamarlo marches away, his back stiff.

"I can't stand this," Alena calls to Jamarlo, but he just keeps going.

"Neither can I," I mutter. "But you know how he can hold a grudge."

"I know." She sighs. Her eyes travel the sidelines and then flick back to me. "Did you see that Matt's here?"

"Yeah. This day keeps getting better."

"Are you okay?"

"Why wouldn't I be?" My jaw tightens. "We only went out for a couple of months."

"Yeah, but he was a jerk at the end. And you were upset after you saw him at Carmen Carter's party last weekend—"

"I don't want to talk about it." Blood thuds in my temples, and I flash back to Carmen's again: Music pounding as I duck into the basement washroom. A shadow on the stairs. Then someone pushing in behind me and slamming the door shut.

Alena gives me a sideways look but says nothing. I'm relieved when she takes her position in net.

I get in a few more practice kicks on Alena, although I'm distracted and miss the net. Then we join the rest of the team for the coach's useless pep talk. "Play to the whistle and keep your eye on the ball," she says, like we don't do that already. When the ref blows the whistle to call the players to the field, I'm jittery and ready to run.

As I head to my position, Melody crosses my path. Even though I don't like her, I decide to warn her. We went to the same soccer boot camp a few times, and I once thought of her as a friend.

I swerve to jog beside her. "Watch out for Matt," I say. "He can get crazy when he drinks."

Melody's pretty nose turns up, and her lips pull into a sneer. "He says the same about you."

As if. I veer away from her, shaken. Has he told her some lie about Carmen's party? I try not to think about it.

"What was that about?" Alena asks when I take my position in front of her.

"Nothing." I squeeze my hands into fists to stop them from trembling. "Melody's being a bitch, as usual."

Unfortunately, the ref tonight is Nick, a balding Italian guy with a moustache who refuses to run with the play and rarely calls offsides—not good when you're up against the Blue Bitches. Then I see Nick offering a flag to Jamarlo so he can be one of the linesmen; they know each other from the guys' league. I start the game feeling like I've got an iron band tightening around my chest.

The Bitches dominate our forwards from the start, blasting the ball into our end. When I stop it with my chest, not caring if it hurts, Melody is in my face in a flash, pulling at my shirt and elbowing me harder than usual. Of course, the ref is too far away to notice her rough play, and the linesmen in our league don't usually call fouls.

"Back off," I growl, shouldering her away from the ball. Warning her about Matt must have brought out her claws.

I kick the ball to our best midfielder, but it's back in our end in seconds. Over and over again, we can't get it much past center.

The next time I get it, Melody grinds her heel into my foot hard enough to make me yell out. Then she runs at Alena with the ball and kicks at the net. Alena dives and then curls her body around the ball.

The play is supposed to end when the goalie's got the ball, but Melody runs right over Alena, kicking into her gut and legs to get the ball loose.

The ref is halfway up the field, oblivious.

"Get the hell off her!" I hobble over on my injured foot, moving through the pain. Going after me during a play is one thing, but kicking Alena when she's down?

Melody lands another kick.

Alena moans, but she refuses to let go of the ball.

I push Melody hard with both hands.

The ref's whistle screams. Finally.

I turn to Nick, ready to hear him ream out Melody for running Alena down after she had the ball.

I get a yellow card in the face.

"Watch it, number 21," Nick says to me.

I get the warning, not Melody? Is he blind?

From the sidelines, my coach protests the call, which is more than she usually does, but Nick ignores her. Jamarlo jogs toward Nick, probably to argue the call, but Nick orders him back to the sidelines.

"Another yellow card and you're out of the game," Nick says to me, like I need to be told the rules by his stupid, lame-assed self. He pulls out a pocket notebook and records my supposed offense.

Jamarlo swings by to check on Alena—who waves him away—before returning to the sidelines with his flag.

Melody is on one knee, getting up slowly as if she's hurt, but I catch the sideways smirk on her face.

I want to scream at Nick, to rant about Melody's dirty tactics, but I clamp my mouth shut so I don't get another card. Then I march over to Alena and help her up.

"You okay?" I ask as a few other Screamin' Demons gather around, swearing quietly at Nick.

Alena leans heavily on me to pull herself up. "Thanks. My knee feels like crap." She winces as she bends it. "But I can still play."

"What is Melody's deal?" I make a fist. My foot still throbs. "Someone should teach her how to play fair."

"Forget about her. She's a jerk." Alena grips my hand. "It's just a game."

"Yeah, I guess you're right." I try to relax. "I just don't want you to get hurt."

Play starts up with a penalty kick against Alena, who dives and misses the ball, probably because of her knee.

1–0. For the Bitches.

A few people on the sidelines cheer. I crush a few weeds with my heel.

My next skirmish with Melody results in an out-of-bounds off her, so we'll get the throw in.

"Blue ball." Jamarlo points the flag in favor of the Blue Bitches.

"What?" I yell at Jamarlo. "The ball went off a Blue player!"

"That's not what I saw." Jamarlo frowns.

Melody smirks.

"Are you talking back now?" Nick jogs over.

"No, sir." I kick at a patch of dirt.

"You better not be." His hand is on his shirt pocket, ready to pull out a card.

"It's fine, Nick." Jamarlo refuses to look at me. Did he call against me on purpose? Or did he really think it was a Blue ball?

Nick blows the whistle for play to resume.

I try to calm down, forget about Jamarlo's call and play by the book—I don't want to risk getting another yellow card.

I'm so busy trying to follow every rule that it's easy for Melody to break free from me and run Alena into the dirt, scoring a second goal for the Bitches.

When the half-time whistle blows, I'm shaking worse than before.

During the break our coach tells us to "Keep up the good work" and then distributes orange slices, as if electrolytes will help against unfair play and biased refereeing.

Beside me, Alena's knee swells to the size of a grapefruit. Meanwhile, across the field, Melody flirts with

Matt as if he's the last man on a dying planet that needs to be repopulated, and Matt plays with her ponytail in the way I used to like. The pulsing in my head intensifies. Somehow, the good memories make it worse.

"Melody can't get away with running you down," I say, passing Alena an ice pack from the coach's cooler.

"Will you just leave it, Tori?" Alena sounds pissed off. Who wouldn't be mad, the way Melody has been going after her?

Then I see Jamarlo laughing with a couple of girls from my team.

"How can he laugh when you're hurt?" I say. "He should be forcing Nick to listen, telling him to call fair."

"Come on, Tori. Jamarlo is only a linesman. You know the ref is always right, even when he's wrong." Alena lifts the ice pack off her knee, bends it and then grimaces.

"Not today." I march toward Jamarlo, but in seconds Alena is beside me, balancing her weight on one foot and yanking me back by the arm.

"I said leave it, Tori!"

"But I'm tired of people bullying us. We should do something—"

"If you convince Jamarlo to talk to Nick, it'll only make things worse. You know refs are egomaniacs, especially Nick."

"Fine." I scowl. "We'll just let Melody terrorize you on the field."

"Tori, don't—" Alena begins, but I walk away from her.

Play starts again, and Melody is in my face worse than ever. When she takes the ball off me yet again, I give up playing nice. I collide with her hard, my elbow out, giving her what she deserves.

Melody lands on the ground, flat on her back.

I pretend that it's no big deal, that I didn't even know it happened. I dribble the ball down the field until Nick's whistle blows, harsh and piercing.

I turn to see Nick staring me down, holding his damn yellow card above his head like a flag.

"It was an accident!" I say. "She had the ball." Why can Melody get away with rough play and I can't?

"Get off the field." His moustache twitches. "Now."

I want to scream at him, argue his call. But instead I stride off, ignoring Melody's smirk, Jamarlo's cold eyes, Alena's concern and the whispers from the other players.

For the rest of the game, I seethe from the sidewalk near where I parked Dad's Civic, since regulations banish me from the park for the rest of the game. Alena gets knocked down and scored on two more times. When Melody is rotated off, she snuggles up next to Matt, who actually seems to like cuddling the sweaty fiend. I make a fist, wishing I could banish Matt from my life.

At the end of the game, Jamarlo helps Alena off the field and over to Dad's car.

"Why didn't you stop Nick?" I say to Jamarlo. "What's wrong with you?" I practically snatch Alena from him.

He just turns away, frowning.

"What's wrong with you, Tori?" Alena pulls back. "You took out Melody on purpose. It's a game, not a battle zone. This is exactly why I left rep."

"What?" I gape at her. "She deserved it! She was a brute for the whole game."

"So were you." Alena hobbles to the passenger side of the Civic. "Let's just forget it. I'm too tired for this."

As I fumble with the door handle, my head pounds. I can't remember Alena ever being mad at me, and I'm not sure how to handle it.

We don't talk. Heaviness settles in my chest. I drop Alena off and head home.

When I get to my room, I get a text from Melody. U had ur chance. Stay away from him.

As if I want to be anywhere near Matt—or her. I toss my phone onto my bed, wishing I'd never given her my number back in boot camp.

Later, in the upstairs bathroom, I lock myself in and dig out Dad's straight razor.

It's not about kids with cancer this time. I'm just not finished with this look yet. It's raw. Strong. Invulnerable.

The lights above the mirror flicker. I end up with only a few nicks at the base of my skull. I climb into the shower and let the water wash the blood away.

HOPE

to wish for something desirable

T he location of Haven Women's Shelter is secret. No one will tell me where it is until after my interview with the director of child care at an offsite office. I also need to undergo a police check—more than a little ironic after the Neanderthal incident.

When I finally learn the address of the shelter, I discover it's on a street near an elementary school where I used to play soccer. Who knew? I feel like I've been granted access to classified information.

I start on May 28 after school. It's the first day of sun after a week of rain—the soccer fields have been waterlogged and slippery. I approach the shelter, curious to see inside and eager to help.

"Do you think working at a shelter is a good idea?"

Mom had said that morning, which translates into *I think it's a bad idea.*

"Why don't you coach a kids' soccer team?" Dad had suggested.

"Why don't you let me make my own decisions?" I replied, which had shut Mom up and made Dad scowl.

The building is at the end of a row of large old homes on a tree-lined street facing the school. Kids' voices echo from the playground. The houses have wide green lawns and bright curtains—the typical cheery display for our suburbs.

The shelter looks like the other houses except for the details. I notice cameras mounted at strategic locations, a high fence with a locked gate to the backyard, and a heavy steel front door. While I'm busy identifying the tell-tale signs, I thud into a man on the sidewalk.

"Watch it!" I frown as my bag slides off my shoulder. Binders and textbooks fall out, pages flapping like clipped wings.

"I'm so sorry." The guy leaps to retrieve my books. He's Dad's age but more clean-cut, with trim fingernails like he's had a manicure.

I squat down to help, feeling I was a little tough on him. "It's all right. I wasn't watching where I was going."

He hands over my books. "Neither was I." His smile seems sincere.

Mr. Manicure saunters away as I shove everything back into my bag. Then I head up the walk, push the buzzer on the intercom and stare at the camera mounted above the door, wondering if I should wave or say my name. Before I can decide, the door clicks open. It's unnerving to walk inside and hear the door clank shut behind me like it's a jail rather than a safe place. It's not these women and kids who need to be locked up.

In the tiny office by the front door, I meet up with Peggy, the director of child care. We met at my interview, when she bombarded me with questions, including *why did you shave your head?* Now she gives me another visual once-over, as if she needs to be reassured I'm good enough. When her eyes land on my shaved head, she purses her lips, which emphasizes the tiny wrinkles around her mouth.

"This is where you'll sign in and out." She points to a clipboard on her desk and reviews the rules with me. "Don't reveal the shelter's location. No photos of the residents. Think of Haven as their home, not a workplace. Any information shared with you about the residents is confidential. Of course, you won't have access to case histories, but our child and youth workers may discuss certain details, if needed." Peggy is all prickles and edges, and I can't help wondering if she ever relaxes.

I'm relieved when she assigns a volunteer named Salvador, who looks about my age, to show me around.

Salvador, who tells me to call him Sal, has dark brown hair, bronze eyes and tan skin. He's tall and thin with arms that hang slack at his sides, as if he doesn't know what to do with them. He walks down the hall with an easygoing lope, leaning backward so that his feet reach the stairs before the rest of him.

We start with the cafeteria-style kitchen in the basement. Sheerma, a tiny woman with a friendly smile and a colorful hijab, is tossing a salad that would be large enough to satisfy even Joel.

"The food is for the residents only, although you can buy a meal if there's extra," Sal says.

Next, he shows me the mothers' program room on the main floor behind the tiny office.

"Most of the moms are out at work or school right now," he says. "But there's group therapy here in the evenings and on weekends. It's also used for classes like yoga, and a hairdresser comes once a month." Sal's warm eyes remind me of a beagle's—calm and kind.

The residents' rooms take up the rest of the main floor and the top floor. In the hall on the second floor, we meet a skittish woman with a black eye, which she's attempted to hide with makeup. She doesn't return my smile.

I peer into the only residents' room that's open as we pass, and I'm shocked by how bare it is. There are bunk beds, one dresser and a lone teddy bear face down in the middle of the floor.

"Why is it so bare?" I ask.

"They probably had to leave home quickly," Sal says. "Get out before they got hurt."

I stiffen, my eyes landing on the abandoned bear. "How do you know so much about this place?"

"I used to live here."

"You what?" Then I get it. He wasn't a volunteer when he lived here. "I'm sorry," I mutter.

"Don't be. This place saved us. It's kinda why I volunteer here now." He ducks his head, so that his hair falls over his eyes, and slouches down the hall toward the stairs.

I get the message and change the subject. "Where are all the kids?"

"Out back. Come on."

There's an empty TV room at the rear of the main floor. The TV is blaring a *Dora the Explorer* episode. Sal switches it off before we push through the doors to a sun-filled addition. I hear the kids before I see them.

"The preschool room's on the left. School-age on the right. You'll be with the school-agers." He gestures at the right-hand door, which is half open, revealing a mini classroom with windows opening onto the fenced backyard.

"Cool," I say, eager to get started.

When I push open the door to step inside, Sal stops me.

"Stay here for a minute," he whispers. "They're just finishing Hope Club."

"What's that?" I whisper back, but Sal just shushes me.

Through the doorway, I see four kids sitting together on the rug in front of a flip chart. A lean Asian woman is writing on the chart paper. They all glance at us briefly, except for a girl with sandy-brown hair who has her hands wrapped around her knees and is staring at her scuffed Nike shoes with such intensity I think they might burst into flames.

"We'll be right with you," the woman says to us. Then she turns to a boy with tight black curls. "What did you say, Jonah?"

"Um, I could draw a picture," he says. "Because I like drawing."

I glance at Sal as if he might explain, but he's watching the kids.

"That's great." The woman writes on the paper.

When I read everything she's written, I press my fingernails into my palms.

When I feel sad I can:
– Hug my mom.
– Talk to a friend.
– Play with my baby brother.

– *Listen to my favorite song.*
– *Draw a picture.*

Thankfully, Hope Club ends before I start to cry.

When Sal and I enter the room, the kids gather around with curious faces, and Sal introduces me to everyone.

Jonah, who is ten years old, is eager to show me how he can lift his little brother Manny, who is seven.

Eleven-year-old Rachel stares at my head before bluntly asking what happened to my hair.

"I cut it off." I smile at her. "It's easier to style."

Casey-Lynn, or Casey for short, is the sandy-haired girl. She's about eight, with large indigo eyes that rarely blink.

And Jia is the child and youth worker I'll be helping.

After a few minutes of chaos and questions about my name, why I'm here and what my favorite color is, Sal goes next door to work with the preschoolers and Jia announces that it's time for journals.

I let the kids pull me to a round yellow table near the windows.

Jia explains that they can write and draw whatever they want in their journals, that it's a time for free expression. Then she says to me, "I'm going to grab a few minutes to work on a report while you sit with them. Okay?"

"Uh, sure," I say, although I'm not sure at all.

The kids dump a basket of pencils and markers on the table and get to work. Jia parks herself in front of the only computer in the room and starts typing.

The journals have lines on one side of the page and space to draw on the other. Beside me, Casey picks up a dark-purple marker and draws a few lines on her blank page, using a ruler to keep the lines straight.

"What are you drawing?" I ask to make conversation.

Casey doesn't say a word. She doesn't even look at me.

I wait, wondering if I said something wrong.

"She doesn't talk." Rachel is printing neatly on the lines.

"Oh?"

"She doesn't want to," Jonah explains. His arms are sprawled across the table, elbows out, as he sketches the outline of some sort of robot.

Casey draws another careful purple line. Her hair falls over her face and onto the paper, but I can see her tongue at the corner of her mouth, tracing the line in the air.

Why won't she talk? Did something terrible happen to her? Instantly, I'm angry, wishing I could do something to help.

I chat with the kids, helping little Manny spell his words and admiring Jonah's alien robot creature and Rachel's story about her imaginary pet dog.

Then Peggy comes to the door to chat with Jia. With one foot in the hall and one in the room, Jia tells me the kids can have free time if they're finished with their journals.

Everyone is done except Casey, who's still drawing heavy purple lines at odd angles.

I'm not sure what to do with the kids, but they don't seem to need my direction. Rachel gets out a well-worn puzzle, and Jonah starts demonstrating to Manny and me how his alien robot creature, named Zambot, knows all the martial arts.

"He's more powerful than Superman and Maximus Prime put together," he says. He raises his fists into protective position and then punches the air in front of him.

It reminds me of self-defense class with Alena.

"Hold your fists a little farther apart." I adjust the position of his hands. "You need to be able to shield your face and stomach."

Manny and Rachel glance at me with curious expressions. Even Casey looks up from her paper.

"How do you know that?" Jonah says, as if my cool factor just increased by fifty points.

"I took a class." I smile.

"Can you teach us?" Manny's on his tiptoes, pulling at my oversized T-shirt. Baggy clothes have become my favorite style.

"I don't know." I glance at Jia, who's deep in a hushed conversation with Peggy. Both of them are standing in the doorway, looking toward the preschool room.

"Please, please, pretty please?" Jonah whines. "Just a little bit?"

"Well, I guess it can't hurt."

I start by explaining that they need to practice on an imaginary person in front of them—they can pretend it's anyone they want as long as they don't practice on each other. Then I teach them the hammerfist, demonstrating how to bring down the side of the fist on a target from above. "Be careful with this one. You can break a nose with it," I say, thinking of Neanderthal.

Casey abandons her purple marker and drops her ruler so it lands half off the table. When she joins us, I smile, watching her bring her tiny fist down hard on whatever imaginary assailant stands before her.

"Nice one," I tell her.

"Look at me," Manny says, before launching his fist in a wild arc that lands on Casey's ruler. It flies over his head toward Casey's horrified face.

"Careful!" I snatch the ruler out of the air, leaving Casey wide-eyed and blinking.

"Whoa!" Jonah gapes.

"Are you a ninja?" Manny asks.

"Don't be dumb." Rachel snorts. "Ninjas aren't real."

"Yes, they are." Manny pouts. "And I'm going to be one when I grow up."

"Are you okay?" I kneel down in front of Casey.

She stares at me for a moment, her eyes like swirling whirlpools, before she gives a slight nod.

"Good." I gingerly pat her shoulder, not sure if she'll shrink away but wanting to reassure her somehow.

"Sorry, Casey," Manny says without prompting.

Jonah executes a perfect hammerfist. "What else can you teach us?"

I'm teaching them the knifehand when I hear Peggy's voice.

"What do you think you're doing?" Her eyes are laser beams.

I step back. "I'm showing them how to defend themselves."

"This is a nonviolent facility. No fighting is tolerated."

"We're not fighting. It's self-defense."

Peggy pinches her lips flat. "I'm not going to debate this in front of the children."

I open my mouth and then shut it again. Family members used to beat up these kids and their mothers, but I'm not allowed to teach them self-defense? Even peacekeepers in war-torn countries are allowed to protect themselves.

My hand muscles twitch, but I force them to relax. "All right," I say.

"Thank you." Peggy's eyes are hard. "We'll review this incident in my office at once."

Great. Why am I always getting lectured these days?

Just as I turn to leave, Casey slips her hand in mine and squeezes.

I stop.

Casey looks up at me with huge pleading eyes.

I glance at Peggy, who nods as if to say, *Take care of the child first.*

"What is it, Casey?" I say, hoping she'll break her silence.

"She wants you to stay," Rachel translates.

Let Casey tell me, I think. I crouch, still holding her hand. "Casey, I have to talk to Peggy now, but I promise I'll be back tomorrow after school." I peek at Peggy, hoping she's not planning on firing me.

Casey frowns.

"And the next day," I add, thinking how I'll take any lecture Peggy throws at me if I can just come back. "And the next." I'm scheduled to help out every day after school, which felt like a lot, until now.

Casey examines my face as if searching for the truth.

When she finally releases my hand, I inhale sharply, hoping Peggy won't make a liar out of me.

CRASH

to execute a spectacular failure

After my first week at the shelter, I ask Alena to meet me at the mall. Ever since she accused me of being like Melody, I've felt disconnected from Alena. I'm hoping we can bond over coffee or window-shopping.

Alena's knee is still too sore to walk far, and I don't want to be reminded of Neanderthal, so we avoid Felipe's Glam Boutique. Instead, we settle for second-rate lattes from McDonald's and sip them at a table in the food court.

The Saturday crowd is as noisy as usual. At a nearby table, there's a little girl with sandy-brown hair who reminds me of Casey, and soon I'm telling Alena all about her.

"Casey won't talk, and she hardly looks at anyone. It's as if she's trying to hide." I lean my elbows on the table with my latte cupped between my hands. "It's like when we were little—when you, me and Jamarlo used to pretend to be invisible. Do you remember?" I try not to miss Jamarlo.

Alena nods. "As long as we didn't move, no one could see us."

"Exactly." I sip my latte, but it's still too hot.

"And your brother used to throw stuff at us to prove we weren't invisible." She grins like it's a good memory.

"Right." I ignore all thoughts of my jerk brother. "When Casey does look at me, she hardly blinks, and I can't look away."

"Is that bad?" Alena blows on her latte to cool it.

"No. I like her. She always gives me a hug when I arrive, and she tugs on my hand when she doesn't want me to leave."

"That's sweet. And you said that she never talks?"

"Not that I've heard, although Sal, this guy I work with, has heard her talk a few times."

"Poor kid." Alena shakes her head. "Do you know what happened to make her so upset?"

"Not really." I hate to think about what Casey may have gone through. "The staff doesn't share too much— only what I need to know to take care of the kids. Casey likes music and books. She smiles when I read to her. And she likes to draw."

"That's good. Sounds like you're helping her." Alena gives me a sincere smile.

"I try to. I've gotten close to all the kids so quickly. They really like me, or maybe they're eager for attention." I sip my drink and relax against the back of the chair. "Don't tell my parents, but it's been fun—except when I almost got fired." I explain what happened when I taught the kids how to do a hammerfist.

Alena's mouth drops open. "You did what? Tori!"

"I know. It was stupid. I endured a half-hour lecture from Peggy before she agreed to keep me on. I tried to explain that I was only teaching the kids to protect themselves. I didn't realize it was a bad idea until Peggy explained that since these kids may have seen violence up close, it can be disturbing for them."

"Well, duh." Alena rolls her eyes. "The stuff we learned in self-defense class wasn't meant for kids."

I swallow hard and abandon my latte on the table. "Why not? Kids can be attacked too. What are they supposed to do if someone comes at them?"

"Run away," Alena says, like she's stating the obvious. "Yell for help. Hide. I don't think you should teach kids to fight."

My head aches. "But what if they're trapped or something? What if no one can hear them? What if there's no place to hide?"

"I don't know, Tori." Alena frowns. "Why are we talking about this anyway?"

"No reason." I jiggle my foot and glance away, feeling nauseated.

She takes a long drink. The silence builds between us.

"How's your knee?" I ask, trying to find a topic we can agree on.

"Not better yet—luckily." Alena's eyes light up.

"You *want* a sore knee?"

"Well, I've been going for physio, and there's this guy who's volunteering there." She wiggles her eyebrows. "I've been wanting to tell you about him."

"You're after a physiotherapist?" I manage a half smile. "Isn't he old?"

"He's only a year older than me; he's a high-school co-op student. We've been out for coffee once. Well, he was doing a coffee run for his bosses, and I was getting a coffee for myself. But we did chat for, like, fifteen minutes before he had to leave." She gets a dreamy look. "You should see his arms!"

"I bet," I say. Alena likes the kind of muscular, sensitive guys who only exist in romance novels. No wonder she's never satisfied with real guys for long.

"And he bought my coffee. Jamarlo says we should—" An uneasy look crosses her face, and she stops talking.

"Jamarlo says you should what?" I assume I'm not included in whatever he's planning.

Alena looks away. "Double-date with him and Carmen Carter."

"Jamarlo and Carmen! Really?" Carmen, who invites sludge like Matt to her parties? If only I'd known what he was like before I dated him. "Why didn't I hear about this?"

Alena fidgets with her cup. "I told you that I don't want to get in between you two. If you want to know what's going on with Jamarlo, ask him."

I shake my head. "He doesn't want anything to do with me."

Alena frowns. "At least you could try to talk to him."

"I guess." I down the rest of my coffee, not wanting to argue with her. It's bad enough that Jamarlo is upset with me. Now Alena and I can't find our groove. How can I get things back to the way they were?

After an awkward silence, I stand up. "I'm going to the washroom. Want to come?" I imagine chatting in front of the mirror while Alena checks her hair.

Alena hoists her sore leg onto my chair. "I don't want to walk that far."

"Sure," I say, trying not to sound disappointed. It's only a washroom run.

I head down the long hallway beside Taco Bell. The harsh fluorescent lights reflect off the glossy white walls and floor. I've almost reached the door to the women's washroom when Matt saunters out of the men's.

My heart leaps into action, pounding double-quick.

Matt grins, lazy and wide. His blue eyes are knife sharp.

"Hey, Tori." His tone is mocking. "Are you looking to hook up in the guys' washroom?" He raises one eyebrow like a question mark.

I recoil like I've been slapped. My head reels. For a horrible second, I'm back in the washroom at Carmen Carter's place. My limbs stiffen in fear.

"Too bad Melody is waiting for me." He smirks before he strolls down the long hall, back toward the food court, which feels like a distant oasis now.

I dive into the washroom. Splash water on my face. Try to still my trembling hands.

When my phone vibrates, it's a text from Matt. Maybe u'll get lucky next time.

Next time?

I huddle in a stall for what feels like ages, trying to calm down, cringing whenever I hear footsteps in the hall. When I'm sure he's long gone, I hurry back to Alena, upset that Matt can reduce me to a quivering lump.

"It's about time," Alena says. "Did you get lost in there?"

I clear my clogged throat. I can hardly think. "Sorry. Let's get out of here."

I offer Alena a ride home, and we head to the Civic without talking. I hold open the mall doors, my hands still shaking, as she limps through.

The sun is intense, like it's summer already. As we take a shortcut between the Dumpsters, we meet up with two girls: a large one in a cut-off jean jacket, and Neanderthal's girlfriend in a tight T-shirt dress.

"Shit," I mutter.

Alena flashes me a worried look and picks up her pace.

The large girl belches loudly, sending the scent of booze toward us. Neanderthal's girlfriend elbows her, leaning close to whisper.

I take Alena's arm and aim her toward the car. When we're several paces past them, the large one calls in a gruff voice, "Hey, you! With the shaved head."

I ignore her.

Behind us, footsteps come closer.

"I'm calling you, Tori Wyatt." The words are slightly slurred.

I know I shouldn't, but I glance back.

The large girl is standing like a bull ready to charge. Neanderthal's girlfriend has her arms crossed. I'm not sure that Alena can make it to the car before this goes sideways.

"Damn, you're as ugly as he said you were," the large girl says. "Your friend too."

I stop. I turn. I inhale the rot from the Dumpsters, my nostrils flaring. Why does she have to be such a jerk?

Alena tugs my arm. "Come on."

"Why'd you shave your head?" the large one says. "Are you a dyke or something?"

Neanderthal's girlfriend smirks.

"Yeah, right. Because every girl who shaves her head must be a dyke." I suck air through my teeth, sick of the idiots who keep harassing me. "Who the hell are you?"

"Jordan Rayfield." She pronounces each syllable like it's a bullet aimed at me. "And you can't just break my cousin's nose and forget about it! Seems fair that I should break your nose now."

I glare at her. "Just try it," I say.

Jordan steps closer, her meaty fists ready. Beads of sweat glisten on her forehead. Her eyes are glassy.

"Let's just go to the car, Tori." Alena yanks my arm harder.

I shake her off. "In a minute." Just one punch. That's all it'll take.

Neanderthal's girlfriend circles behind me, where I can't see her. Would she try to get in on the action? I try to keep both of them in sight.

"You don't have to do this, Tori." Alena has her phone out now. "Just walk away." She backs toward the car.

Jordan snorts. "You won't walk away from this." She sideswipes my ear when I glance at Neanderthal's girlfriend.

Alena yelps. Pain shoots through my head and bounces off the opposite sides of my skull.

"Try that again when I'm looking." I'm sick of people who don't fight fair.

I ready my fists in front of me in a protective position, but I'm not there long.

Jordan and I dive at each other.

I land two good hits in Jordan's gut and try to block as she aims for my head. Wham. Another blow to the same ear.

With my head still vibrating, I recoil my arm, winding up for my next punch. Jordan steps back against a grease-coated Dumpster. I let go with all my strength.

Jordan dodges.

My fist smashes into the side of the Dumpster.

I howl as pain spikes through my fingers and up my arm.

"Leave her alone!" Alena screams, cell phone to her ear.

Jordan laughs. "You beating yourself up, Tori?"

Neanderthal's girlfriend covers her smile with one hand.

I fold my arm against my chest. The pain makes my head spin and my eyes water. My legs are unsteady as I turn to face Jordan, desperate to fend off the next blow.

I skid on a slick of grease. One leg collapses. I crack my head against the Dumpster as I fall.

"Christ, Tori!" Alena yells.

I crash to the pavement, head roaring. The sky fades to black.

PiPED

*to get hit by a lead pipe
(or feel like you were)*

I wake up flat on my back, staring at industrial ceiling tiles. The ache in my head is explosive. A killer pain shoots through my right hand. The air smells like disinfectant.

Where am I?

My muscles scream as I try to sit up.

I glimpse floor-to-ceiling blue curtains. When a hand on my shoulder pushes me back down, I wince. My head lands on a pillow.

Then a face comes into view. Warm, brown eyes. A sympathetic smile. A nurse's uniform. Her lips move. "You're in the emergency department at Glencrest Hospital. Try to relax."

Relax? I remember Jordan's fist coming at me. Me punching the Dumpster and then tripping. A vague recollection of sirens and an EMS uniform. My cheeks burn.

"My friend—Alena Kostakos." I grip the metal side bars on my bed and try to sit up again, even though I'm light-headed. "Is she okay?" Would Jordan have turned on Alena after I knocked myself out?

"She's in the waiting room with your family," she says. "And she's fine, as far as I can tell. She's very concerned about you."

I exhale sharply.

"You can see them soon," she continues. "Dr. Balestra will want to check you over again, now that you're alert."

The nurse hustles out through an opening in the curtains, clipboard in hand. Beyond the curtain, I can hear whispered conversations, footsteps, a long moan and the beep of machines.

I prop myself up with the pillow, even though every move feels like a fresh punch. I'm still wearing my T-shirt and jeans, although my shoes are gone. I feel a gauze bandage on the side of my head. My right hand is swollen. Wiggling my little finger hurts so much my eyes water.

A few minutes later a doctor comes in and introduces herself. Dr. Balestra is young, with black hair in a ponytail and a brief smile. She gets right to work, gently prodding my head and neck, checking my reflexes and asking if I know my own name and what day it is.

"I can remember everything," I tell her. Every embarrassing detail.

She asks penetrating questions about how I got my injuries, which I answer as briefly as possible. I'm not proud of punching a Dumpster.

"Was there a weapon involved?" She probes my tender left ear, the one Jordan hit twice.

I flinch. "No. Why would you ask that?"

"It's procedure." She tucks a stray lock of hair behind her ear as she bends over to examine the swollen fingers of my right hand. "I need to know whether to get the police involved. It seems like this other girl laid into you pretty hard. We can call the police if you want."

"No." My tone is firm. "It's over." Ever since Neanderthal threatened to call the police, I've wanted nothing to do with them. Anyway, how could I charge Jordan when I punched the Dumpster? I'm such an idiot.

"Your choice." She's still examining my hand. Then she says, "Well, you're lucky. Your injuries seem minor."

"I don't feel lucky."

"It all depends on your point of view." She smiles. "You have a concussion. The prolonged loss of consciousness is a concern, but you seem to have no memory loss, slurred speech or other symptoms. We'll run further assessment tests and get your parents to keep an eye on you for the next forty-eight hours, but you should be fine. As for your hand…"

She touches it, and the pain is so bad I want to retch.

"I suspect a boxer's fracture."

"A what?"

"A broken bone at the base of the small finger in the metacarpal neck, which extends from the wrist to the knuckle at the base of the finger." She points.

"Don't touch it." I shrink back.

"Okay. But we're going to need to set it." She pats my knee, one place on my body that doesn't hurt. "The injury is typical for boxers, usually resulting from a straight punch. Is that what happened?"

I nod and look away.

"That's why there's so much swelling near the knuckle of your little finger. And this bump below the knuckle is likely the break point. Of course, we'll need to get an X-ray to confirm it."

"Will I need a cast?"

She nods. "I can get you a soft cast. It's removable so you can shower. But I recommend no more punching, no high-impact sports, no weight-lifting—"

"What about soccer?"

"No way." She shakes her head. "If you push this injury early, it'll make it worse in the long run. And you need to protect your head from further trauma. It can take weeks or months for a brain to heal. Better to take care and be patient."

"Great." I sigh. Just wait until the girls on my team hear about this.

Just then Alena pushes through the curtains, followed by my parents and even Joel. He was probably out with them when they got Alena's call.

I could do without Joel, but I'm happy to see Alena—finally. She's acting chummy with my parents, linking arms with them.

"I was afraid this would happen." Mom untangles from Alena to grip my good hand, squeezing hard.

"How bad is it?" Dad's face is pale.

"I'm fine," I tell them after Dr. Balestra introduces herself again.

Joel takes one look at my swollen hand and says, "What'd you do—punch a Dumpster?" Mr. Sensitive doubles up, laughing.

I frown. Of course everyone would know. Alena's never been able to lie to my mother.

"That's enough," Mom says.

"Go wait in the hall, Joel," Dad barks.

"It's a joke! Don't you get it?" Joel takes one look at Dad's flaming face and backs up. "Sorry, sibling," he says without prodding from Mom or Dad before he wanders out. Could Joel be developing empathy?

As soon as Joel leaves, Mom hones in on me.

"I just don't understand how you got into another fight." Mom pinches her lips together. "Why do you keep putting yourself in danger? I think you may need to talk to a therapist, Tori."

"No, Mom. It won't happen again, really," I plead, feeling awkward in front of Alena and the doctor.

"Well, the important thing is that you're going to be okay." Dad turns to Dr. Balestra. "She is going to be okay, isn't she?"

The doctor answers all their questions while I'm stretched out on display. I'm glad when my parents stop fussing over me to go sign some forms with the doctor.

"At least we all agreed not to press charges." I snort.

Alena frowns at my swollen hand. She dabs at the makeup under one eye, and I wonder if she's getting teary over me.

"You can sit, if you want." I slide over to make room on the bed for her, even though it hurts to move.

"I don't want to sit," Alena says, and I notice the tight line of her mouth.

"What's wrong?" I ask. "Did Jordan hurt you?"

"What? No! Because I didn't pick a fight with her."

"But I wasn't—"

"Really, Tori? I know what I saw. These days, if anyone crosses your path, you fight them."

"It's not like that."

"But it is! Just like with that guy at the mall and Melody. It's like you think you're the Incredible Hulk, raging against anyone who pisses you off." She flips her dark hair over one shoulder. "I don't understand what's happening with you!"

"So I should have done nothing?" I lift my head off the pillow, my neck straining. "Just let Jordan hit me? Should I also have let Melody run you down? And Neanderthal taunt Jamarlo?"

"You should have avoided it all! We could have made it to the car—I'm not that slow. Or headed back into the mall. Or called for help. You didn't have to hurt yourself."

I drop back down on the pillow, scowling. "I have the right to defend myself," I say, but I wonder if she's right. Maybe I'm too wound up to think clearly.

"Of course you do. But you're not the Hulk, Tori. You're as breakable as the rest of us."

"I figured that out." I raise my right hand off the blanket.

"So why do you keep getting into fights? I mean, this is me, Tori. You can tell me what's going on."

"I don't know." I sigh heavily, lowering my hand. "I guess I'm just..." I pause, searching for words. "Trying to stand up to the idiots I meet."

"Seriously?" Alena gives me a skeptical look. "Why?"

"Why not?" We lock eyes. Her gaze is intense. Searing. I refuse to look away. How do I tell her that I'm trying to be strong so I don't feel weak? That I can't talk about Matt because I can't stand feeling helpless?

The nurse sweeps back the curtains around my bed. "Time for X-rays." She pushes a wheelchair closer.

"I'll see you later then." Alena shoots me a final, penetrating glance. "Call me when you get home."

"You're leaving?" I try not to sound surprised. A month ago, both Alena and Jamarlo would have been at my bedside until the hospital released me.

"I have homework. Exams are soon, you know. Take care of yourself, Tori. I mean it." She disappears into the hall.

The gap between Alena and me widens. It hurts more than my hand, but I don't know how to fix it.

∽

I'm at the hospital for hours. Mom and Joel left after only an hour, heading to Glencrest Mall to pick up the Civic. That was after Mom and Dad lectured me for thirty minutes about the perils of fighting and the joys of alternative conflict resolution. Ironic coming from Dad, the former bouncer. Alena hasn't even texted to see how I am.

Because I have a concussion, I have to rest, and my broken hand will be in a cast for four to six weeks. The cast is a removable black sleeve that holds my pinky and ring fingers rigid at a weird angle, although I can sort of use the other fingers and thumb. I'm not looking forward to telling my soccer team that I can't play until the cast is off, and maybe not even then.

As Dad and I push open the hospital doors, I'm tired, sore and relieved to escape. The smell of disinfectant has seeped into my clothes, and I just want to collapse into bed. Outside, the air smells like flowers and the sun is still high in the sky, even though it's evening. The days are getting longer, but I still feel a heavy shadow over me.

Dad parked the SUV on a side street, since the lot was full. As we shuffle down the sidewalk, he finishes the last of his hospital food—his second hamburger. Joel would be going for his third.

A magnolia tree has littered the sidewalk with petals. Two kids skateboard by. Cars race along the street.

That's when I notice the black squirrel at the side of the road. He's splayed on his back, breathing hard in and out, his eyes glazed.

I stop, horrified.

A car must have hit him. I clench my jaw. What kind of person just abandons an animal when it's helpless and injured, gasping for breath?

Joel would poke it with a stick. Mom would tell me to keep my distance. Dad just keeps walking.

"Hurry up," he calls. "Your mother's making dinner."

My throat tightens.

Then Dad glances back and notices the squirrel.

"Oh, Tori." He sighs. "There's nothing we can do."

I stand motionless, watching the squirrel take its dying breaths.

When the squirrel goes limp, a large bubble lodges in my throat. I try to gulp it down and hiccup instead. The bubble stays, choking me.

"We can't leave it here," I finally manage to say.

"You need to get home and rest." Dad frowns. "Besides, your mother will kill me if you touch it."

"It's not diseased." I glare at him. "It was murdered."

His eyes soften. "I have a plastic bag in the truck. You can use that to pick it up."

FLUTTER

to move quickly and nervously

Dad digs a hole in our backyard garden, near the day lilies. I grip the bag that holds the dead squirrel with my good hand.

I remember the squirrel's eyes, glassy and vacant. I can't stop my hands from trembling.

Dad leans on the shovel. "Deep enough?"

The earth smells like worms and decay. I nod, take a deep breath and lower the squirrel, bag and all, into the hole.

We don't talk while he shovels earth over the squirrel. I feel like I should say something about how this squirrel should have been leaping through trees and munching seeds, not mowed down by some uncaring asshole, but that bubble lodges in my throat again.

When Dad squeezes my shoulder with his big hand, I want to dive into his arms. I remember Dad, solid and warm, holding me after I fell off my bike and scraped my forehead when I was seven. But I'm not a little girl anymore, and he can't fix what's wrong.

"Now will you go inside and rest?" he asks.

A wave of exhaustion hits me. "Sure," I say.

We head inside. I skip Mom's dinner of leftovers and collapse between my cool cotton sheets. I just want to sleep, but instead I stare at the last of the sunlight that filters through my blinds and across the clothes on the floor. My hand aches no matter how I hold it, and my brain won't stop cycling through my memories of the day.

Eventually, I text Alena—at least I can still type with my good fingers. I tell her that my right hand is broken. No response. I leave a message for my soccer coach, saying that I can't play for a few weeks, but I'll still come to the games.

Then I get a random text from Melody. what did I tell u? Stay away from him, slut.

What the hell? Did Matt tell her he saw me at the mall? Was she watching us? Does she still think I'm after him? Whatever is going on in her stupid, jealous brain, I just want to forget Matt. Can't Melody and everyone else let me do that?

I finally sleep, but I awaken to pain in the middle of the night, sure that Matt is twisting my fingers into new, agonizing shapes. *You know you want it, Tori*, he whispers in my ear. I'm gasping, and then I realize that I'm lying on top of my hand, crushing the bruised fingers. I stay awake for hours, eyeing the shadows in the corners of my room, feeling like the night has a tight grip on my throat.

On Sunday, my aches seem even worse and fresh bruises bloom. I convince Mom to let me miss school the next day. I'd rather do homework and watch bad daytime TV than answer a billion questions about my hand and the cut above my ear. But no way will I miss any of my shifts at the shelter.

⤳

Monday is the first stiflingly hot day since last summer. I find the kids in the fenced backyard of the shelter. The air rings with joyful shrieks as Rachel, Jonah and Manny run through a spinning typhoon of a sprinkler, colliding with one another and sliding on the slick grass.

Sal is there too, with his crew of preschoolers and the other child and youth worker, Francine.

Casey hangs back by the shed, her eyes on the spray. She's the only kid not in a bathing suit, but at least her feet are bare. I watch her dip one toe in a puddle on the soggy grass. When the other kids notice me, I'm swarmed. Manny latches onto my middle, soaking my T-shirt and shorts.

Two preschoolers I don't know well copy him, and my bruises ache anew. Jonah shows me his new blue-and-red-striped bathing suit. Rachel pokes a finger at my cast, demanding to know what happened.

"I ran into a garbage can," I tell Rachel. I don't want to lie, but I'm not sharing details either.

"How?" Manny's eyes cloud with worry. "Did you trip?"

"Sort of." I think about how his mother may have tried to hide injuries to her body. "But I'm okay, Manny."

He nods, his eyes serious.

Casey wanders over, her eyes on my cast. She lingers in the background, as usual, waiting for the excitement to die down.

"Can we sign your cast?" Rachel pleads. A drop of water dangles from the tip of her nose, and her long hair hangs in snaky clumps.

"It's not the signing kind. Sorry." I tap it. "See? It's covered in cloth. And it's black, so the writing won't show."

Rachel's face falls briefly and then brightens. "I'll make a card for you instead." She hurries away, and I can hear her telling Jia that I broke my hand so she needs paper and pencils to make a get-well card for me.

When the other kids run back to the sprinkler, Casey gives me a fleeting hug.

"How are you, Casey?" I say, hoping today will be the day she answers me.

But she just gives me her usual wounded, wide-eyed stare and then wanders back to flutter near the other kids.

The heat of the sun makes my hand sweat inside my cast. I retreat to the shade, where Sal slouches against the trunk of a maple, the one tree that towers over the yard.

"Hey," he says. "Too bad about your hand."

His heavy bangs fall across his eyes and swoop to one side. His smile is soft, and I like how he doesn't ask nosy questions. I could get to like this guy, except I'm off the market.

"Thanks. Where's Ethan today?" I ask. Ethan is a chubby two-year-old Sal often has in tow.

"He moved out."

"Of the shelter? Where did he go?"

"I don't know exactly." He leans one tanned foot against the tree trunk. "Francine said that his family finally got into subsidized housing. They've been on the list for a year."

"He's just gone? That quickly?" I'd want to say goodbye before any of my kids left.

"Yup," he says, like he's used to people disappearing. "They're lucky."

Then two preschoolers start a tug-of-war over a sit-and-scoot car, and Sal lopes over to settle it.

I wander over to Casey to encourage her to go in the sprinkler. Together, we let the sprinkler spray our bare feet. I can't go in farther because I need to keep my cast dry.

When Casey strips to her bathing suit and edges closer to the sprinkler, I return to the shade to find Sal holding a monarch butterfly. It's perched on his hand, opening and shutting its wings every so often. One wing is torn in half.

"Where'd you get that?" The sight of this tall guy cradling an injured butterfly makes me strangely emotional.

"It was just sitting in the sunshine on the slide, and I didn't want the kids to run over it." He points to the playground, which has a low red slide for the preschoolers. "Don't monarchs migrate?"

I nod. "Maybe that's how it tore its wing. I hope it can still fly." I try not to think about what will happen to it if it can't. "It's amazing how something that frail can be so strong."

"It must have flown to get here." He holds the butterfly up near his face to examine it, and the butterfly waves its antennae in front of his nose. "Maybe it flew through the sprinkler. It could be too wet to fly."

"Maybe." I glance over at the kids and get a great idea. "Hold on a minute. I'll be right back."

I approach Casey, who's tramping gently over the water-soaked grass, looking back at her footprints.

"Casey, come here for a second."

Casey's eyes grow wider when she spies the butterfly. Sal kneels and slowly extends his hand. The butterfly opens its black-and-orange wings.

"Sal found it," I explain. "It probably flew thousands of miles to get here. It must be the first to arrive this spring. Pretty cool, huh?"

Her eyes don't leave the butterfly. "Can I hold it?" she asks.

My mouth falls open. Sal and I exchange a glance. I swallow my excitement and say, "Sure. Just be careful not to touch its wings—it's really fragile."

"I'll be careful," she says.

I marvel at her sweet, lilting voice.

She holds her pale fingers next to Sal's. It takes a while, but eventually the butterfly rests on her hand.

Casey sucks in a breath. "Wow," she whispers. Her eyes blaze.

Sal gives me a way-to-go grin and then takes off to help a preschooler who is teetering at the top of the slide. I talk to Casey about butterflies, migration, cocoons and so on, thrilled every time she answers. Jia joins the conversation, raising her eyebrows at me.

After a while, Casey wanders away with the butterfly perched on her hand. I can hear her whispering to it, but I can't make out what she's saying. I love the contented smile on her face.

"I don't know how you got her to talk, Tori." Jia pats me on the back. "But whatever you did, keep doing it."

"I just showed her the butterfly," I say.

"It's more than that, Tori. Casey feels comfortable with you."

"Really?" I stand a little taller.

"Yes. Now please tell me what happened with the butterfly. Her mother will want a full report."

I tell her everything. As I finish, Rachel lets out a shriek.

"Casey has a butterfly," she announces. "Where'd you get it?"

Soon there's a crowd around Casey. Jia and I head over.

"Tori and Sal gave it to me," Casey says.

None of the kids seem surprised to hear her speak.

"Can I have one too?" Manny glances at me pleadingly, like I might have another one stashed behind my back.

"Sal only found one." I smooth Manny's wild hair. "Sorry."

"Can I hold it?" Rachel is more direct.

"I want a turn." Jonah stomps his foot.

"It's not a good idea to pass it around," Jia says. "It's a living creature, not a toy. And it's hurt." She points. "See the broken wing? It may not be able to fly."

"That's okay." Casey's voice is steady. "Because I'm going to keep Monty safe. He can stay with me."

"Monty?" I grin.

"Is that his name?" Jonah asks.

"We can all feed him." Rachel pushes closer.

The butterfly closes its wings.

I'm just about to tell the kids to give the butterfly some space when Casey says, "Not too close. You'll scare him." She cups her hand around the butterfly and beams at me.

I give her a thumbs-up.

Casey holds the butterfly near her chest. The other kids visit and then wander back to the sprinkler. Soon the moms start trickling into the backyard. I've gotten to know a few of them since they come to collect their kids before dinner each night.

Casey's mom, Rita, talks to Jia and then hurries over. I'm proud and slightly embarrassed when she thanks me repeatedly for encouraging her daughter to talk.

"You know, Casey-Lynn really admires you." Rita has dark circles under her eyes, and she looks exhausted. "Last night in our room, she was talking about you."

"That's great. I like her too." I smile, staring at Rita's face and trying to decide why it looks so lopsided today.

"So many people at the shelter have helped us, but you..." She pauses to gaze intently at me. "Somehow you connect with Casey so well."

"I guess." When I realize that she only has makeup on one eye, I marvel at how she could forget to do the other eye. Is she too busy? Too stressed? Jia had once asked Rita how the search for an apartment was going; apparently, it's hard to find an affordable one these days.

Just then I hear a horrible screech from across the yard.

I turn to see Casey falling to her knees, wailing. Her arm stretches toward the sky as the butterfly flits away, wobbling above the shed, over the fence and beyond.

Her mother runs to her. I stare after the butterfly, silently pleading for it to come back.

∾

I don't want to leave the shelter until Casey calms down. She sits between her mother and me on the hard bench in the yard, sniffling and wiping her nose every so often. When her mother brings out their dinner, Casey hardly eats.

Eventually, I say, "I have to go soon, Casey." Exams are coming, and I've barely started any of my review packages. The sun has set behind the trees, although the sky is still bright.

"Not yet." Casey's eyes get watery. She wraps her arms around my neck.

"I'll go in five minutes." I hold her shivering body. "But first, I want to tell you something."

"What?" She pulls back and examines my face.

I glance at Rita, who looks drained. "Today I'm sad and happy at the same time," I say.

Casey shoots me a confused look.

"I'm sad because when the butterfly left, you cried. Maybe if I hadn't shown him to you, you wouldn't be hurting now."

"But I loved Monty!"

"I know. And I loved showing him to you. That's why I'm happy. Because when you saw the butterfly, you spoke to me." I smile. "I like when you talk."

"You do?"

"Yup. I like it so much that right now, my happy feelings are bigger than my sad ones."

"I like talking to you too." She throws her arms around me again, but this time she's not shaking.

I give Casey a final hug and disentangle from her.

Rita nods at me. "Thank you again. I seem to be saying that a lot to you today."

"I like helping." I shrug, embarrassed. Then I say to Casey, "Talk to you tomorrow?"

"Okay." She wipes her eyes.

Ten minutes later I head out the back gate, which opens onto the sidewalk. I've got Rachel's hastily scribbled card in hand; she wanted to get back to the sprinkler more than she wanted to draw. Across the street, Mr. Manicure, the tidy neighbor with the trim fingernails, is cutting the grass with a noisy electric lawn mower. Apparently, he prunes his yard as well as he trims his nails. When he sees me coming, he waves and turns off the motor.

I wave back and keep walking.

"You work at the shelter?" he calls across the street.

He knows it's a shelter? I try not to show my surprise.

He grins, heading across the street toward me, stripping off his gardening gloves one at a time. "We all know it's a shelter. I mean, look at the cameras." He points to the one above the gate to the backyard. "It's pretty obvious."

I glance at the shelter and then back at him, feeling uncomfortable. He's right, but Peggy told me not to talk about it. *For the safety of the residents*, she said.

"Yeah, I know all the people there." He steps too close, and I can smell his musky aftershave mixed with the scent of gasoline. "Peggy Epstein tells me about them. Rachel is a sweet girl, and Casey too. Do you know them?"

I step back. Is this guy a creep or just sickeningly nice? "Uh, I've got to go." I hurry away without glancing back.

"Okay. Bye, Tori."

Did I tell him my name?

From now on, I'll be avoiding that guy.

CONCEAL

to keep secret

Getting ready for school the next day is worse than usual.

Joel takes more than his share of time in the bathroom, and when I do get into the stinky, soggy mess he leaves behind, I slip on the wet floor and whack my sore hand on the edge of the counter. I can't easily shave my head with my broken hand, even though my hair is growing in. In front of the mirror, I find that my concealer refuses to hide the cut over my left ear.

Dad has already left for his shift, and I'm waiting for Mom to holler up at me to come for breakfast. When she squeezes into the bathroom with me, I'm surprised.

"Are you going to be okay today?" she asks.

She's wearing dress pants with a neat crease down each leg, high heels and a freshly ironed shirt. She smells like perfume and coffee, and in the mirror beside me, her makeup is good enough to make me feel like a preteen trying to do my face for the first time.

I dodge around her to grab my concealer off the counter. "Why wouldn't I be?" I dab more on the cut and blend it in. I don't want people yapping about it at school. I'm wearing a loose, long-sleeved black shirt that hides most of the cast, even though it's warm again today.

My mother smooths in the concealer behind my ear.

I jerk away. "I can do it."

"I know." She frowns at me in the mirror. "Just stay out of trouble today. Dad and I don't know what to expect from you next. I still think a therapist would be a good idea."

"Forget it, Mom." I roll my eyes. "There's nothing to worry about."

"Is that so? You hardly eat anymore. You're withdrawn, and you're always preoccupied." She waggles her school-teacher finger at me. "Maybe you're having trouble with something or someone? Maybe a boy? If you won't talk to a therapist, you could at least talk to me about whatever's going on with you."

In the mirror, my face goes white. "I'm fine, Mom." Like I'd ever talk to her about Matt.

She studies me and then glances at her watch. "I have to get to school. We'll talk later," she says, like it's decided.

Not if I can help it.

I endure the kiss she plants on the top of my head and lock the bathroom door after she leaves. I know she means well, but my mother talks more than she listens, and she's a control freak. The middle-school kids she teaches don't dare cross her, and at home she runs our lives too. Sometimes I can handle it, but mostly I just want her to let me live my own way.

I sweep my concealer off the counter and into my makeup drawer. I hope this lousy start to the day isn't a sign of what's to come.

∽

As I'm heading toward World History, sweating in my cast and long-sleeved shirt, I see Jamarlo with Carmen, who's in my class. She's dressed in a faded jean jacket, white jean cutoffs and ripped black tights. He's in a leopard-print hoodie, jeans and his trademark fedora. They're melded together in a parting kiss, with her hand on his waist and his arm stretched to her shoulder, since she's taller than him. She's leaning down to reach his lips.

Since I have to walk right past them, I figure, what the hell? Why not break the silence?

I tug my sleeve down lower over my cast and say, "Hey, Jamarlo."

Maybe I call to him out of habit. Maybe I just miss him too much.

I keep walking, since I don't want to hassle them or deal with Jamarlo's wrath, but before I get much distance between us, Jamarlo and Carmen pull apart, looking startled.

Carmen blinks rapidly, as if she's just waking up. "Check out that cast!" she says, disentangling from Jamarlo and drying her lips on the back of her hand.

"Whoa!" Jamarlo says, as if he hasn't been refusing to talk to me for weeks. "What happened to your arm?" He plays with Carmen's bobbed, white-blond hair, twirling it between his fingers like he's proud to have access.

"Uh…it's my hand." I'm thrown off by how easy it was to get him to talk to me. "I slipped on the soap," I lie. "Showering is a dangerous occupation."

"Did you hit your head too?" Carmen points to the cut above my ear. Obviously, my concealer is failing.

"Uh, shaving accident," I say.

"Yeah?" Jamarlo links fingers with Carmen and tugs her closer. He glances up and down the hall as if he's checking out who's noticing them together.

"Uh, yeah." I'm glad he's got a girlfriend, but he could at least pay attention to me when I'm trying to make up with him.

Carmen cracks her gum. I don't want to know where she stashed it when they were making out. "I never got why you shaved your head," she says.

Carmen can be tacky and insensitive, like when she told Alena that she would be pretty if she wore more makeup. I also blame Carmen for inviting Matt to her party. But I'll endure her for Jamarlo.

"Just a haircut that got out of hand," I say.

"Tori likes the tough-girl look." Jamarlo grins, but his tone has a raw edge to it. "She thinks she can beat up guys twice her size." He pretends to punch me.

I pretend to duck. It's our usual game, even if it feels a bit off. "Size doesn't matter." I keep my tone playful, teasing. "You should know that, Jamarlo."

Carmen laughs. Jamarlo loses his grin. I guess we're not back to joking yet.

"I'm kidding, Jamarlo." I force a laugh too, but it sounds as if I'm choking.

"I know that." His dark eyes are on mine. He frowns.

"Yeah, well," I manage to say, "I've got to get to class. See you later."

He nods, still frowning.

I duck into World History and head to the back of the room. What just happened? Jamarlo and I may be talking again, but we're not okay.

A few minutes later, Carmen enters the room and slides into a seat beside me. I wish she'd sit somewhere else, but I'm not that lucky.

"Settle down, class." Mr. Hadley pulls down the screen at the front of the room. "Today we're going to talk about some of the key passive-resistance movements that occurred after 1945."

I usually like Mr. Hadley's discussions, but today I'm hoping for a long movie so I can think about what happened with Jamarlo.

Carmen leans over to me and whispers loud enough for others to hear, "So do you and Matt want to come over this weekend? Jamarlo and I are having a few couples to my place since my parents are away."

Hell, no.

My throat goes dry. I swallow hard. "We broke up," I say. Obviously, Jamarlo hasn't been sharing info about me.

Mr. Hadley sits on the edge of his desk. "The best-known movements are those led by Mahatma Gandhi in India, Martin Luther King Jr. in the United States and Nelson Mandela in South Africa. More recently, the 2011 Egyptian revolution used a campaign of civil resistance to overthrow President Hosni Mubarak."

"Yeah, but we can fix that." Carmen winks. "Matt's a nice guy."

Nice guy? My hands clench, but it hurts my sore fingers. I get a flash of our first date, when he took me to the Keg for dinner. Matt insisting on opening the car door for me. Matt raving about my gorgeous hair to the hostess, the waiter, anyone who would listen. Matt trying to order for me. Matt going on about how he's going to be a vet—he adores animals too—and I could be his assistant. Then, I was flattered that he'd even noticed me. I didn't know he thought he owned me.

Mr. Hadley is still talking about nonviolent conflicts. "We'll be watching a video called *A Force More Powerful* over the next few classes, but first I want to talk about how Gandhi resisted British rule. Who can tell me what they know about it?"

As Mr. Hadley tries to extract answers from the class, Carmen starts whispering about how sexy Matt is and how she used to have a crush on him in middle school.

"Anyway," she continues, "Jamarlo really wants you to come. Alena and her new guy may be there. Maybe I can hook you up with someone else?"

"No, thanks," I say through gritted teeth. Is Alena with her physio guy now?

Mr. Hadley appears in front of our desks.

"I assume you girls are sharing your thoughts about Gandhi's resistance movement?" He taps his pen against my unopened binder.

A few people laugh.

Carmen chomps on her gum and says nothing.

I sink low in my seat. I like Mr. Hadley, so it feels rotten to be scolded by him.

"I thought so. Pay attention, girls." He wanders to the front of the room, explaining how Gandhi opposed the British by declaring a law unjust and then purposely breaking it, letting himself and his followers suffer arrest, physical abuse and even prison. "The idea was that, ultimately, the oppressors would get the message and do what's right."

Yeah, sure. I snort.

Because I've seen assholes suddenly change their ways so many times. In the meantime, more people get hurt. The way I see it, it's not okay to sacrifice anyone.

Mr. Hadley dims the lights and puts on the video. As I watch Gandhi's nonviolent struggle, I can't stop thinking about Matt, Neanderthal, Melody and Jordan. According to the video, violence is not the ultimate form of power.

I wish that were true.

After the video I'm left wondering, what if the oppressors never get the message?

Sometimes you have to stop them, any way you can.

BAiL

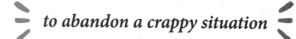

to abandon a crappy situation

After my shift at the shelter, I'm supposed to meet up with Alena at a bus stop in our neighborhood. Dad has this crazy idea that I can't drive his car with a broken hand. We're heading to soccer, me to watch and her to play, even with her sore knee. I'm not looking forward to sitting on the sidelines.

The bus comes, but Alena doesn't. When I phone her, it goes to voice mail. I wave the driver on and worry. I couldn't find Alena at lunch either. Is she avoiding me?

I sit in the shade of the nearest house to get out of the sun. The short grass prickles my bare legs, making them itch. My cast is hot. I phone Alena four more times. Her voice mail pisses me off. Maybe she forgot about me.

Alena keeps me waiting ten more minutes. She arrives breathless, running with a hop and a skip to favor her strong leg, her soccer bag slung over her shoulder and a brace around her sore knee. Her hair is in a high ponytail, and her cheeks are flushed.

"Sorry." She smiles like she means it. "I got home late and I've been rushing ever since."

"What's wrong with your phone?"

"Nothing." Her eyes sparkle in the sunlight. "I was on the phone with Daniel, the guy from physio, for an hour!"

I can tell she's bursting with news, but first I want to know if she's been avoiding me.

"Where were you at lunch?" I try to keep my voice light. "I looked for you in the caf and outside."

She squeezes my good arm. "I met Daniel at the burger place near Mill Pond."

"Oh," I say, knowing how obsessed Alena can get when she's into a guy.

"It's halfway between our schools. He goes to the Catholic school."

The same school Matt goes to.

"I missed the whole afternoon. He bought some bread at a corner store and we went to Mill Pond Park to feed the geese. It was wonderful!"

I open my mouth to rant about how bread is bad for geese, but I don't want to start another fight. So I just say, "Well, you could have told me." How long does it take to send a text?

"I know. Sorry—again! I just forgot about everything. This guy is different than any other guy I've met. He's… special. You know?" She tucks her arm into mine and beams. "My father is mad that I forgot to walk the dogs. Don't you be mad at me too." Alena has two pugs that stay locked up in the house until she comes home.

"It's all right," I say, even though it isn't. She hasn't asked about my hand since the hospital.

I'm about to tell her that Casey spoke to me for the first time yesterday, and that she's still speaking today, but Alena starts going on about how glad she is that Jamarlo and I are talking again. "He and Carmen told me all about it! I hope this means you're back to your old self again."

"Uh, sure," I say, even though I'm not sure at all.

"Good." Alena checks the time on her phone. "Do you think we'll be late for the game?" She peers down the street for the bus. "Daniel said he'd come to watch me play."

"That's great." I try to sound happy for her. It's just that guys aren't always who you think they are.

"I might invite him to the anti-prom. Wouldn't it be fun to go with someone—like on a date, I mean?"

Not that I want to go, but she used to be begging me to go with her.

"Yeah," I say. "You'd have a great time."

I'm the only girl on my team not in uniform. The only girl not warming up.

We arrive just as the Screamin' Demons start running the perimeter of the field. Alena quickly introduces me to Daniel, blushing and giggling the whole time. Daniel is six feet tall and muscular, with wavy brown hair and stubble. Exactly Alena's type.

"What do you think?" she whispers when we leave to join our team.

"He seems like a nice guy," I say. He kept his eyes on my face—not like some guys, who talk to my chest.

"I know!" She squeals and then hurries to catch up with the rest of our team.

When they form a circle to do stretches, I wander over, trying not to think about how I'm letting them down.

"Are you sure you can't play?" a defender named Marla asks. Last game, she worked my left side, and she was good at digging the ball out of the corners and shooting it up the out-of-bounds line to the midfielders.

"Sorry." I shake my head, feeling worse.

"We're gonna get creamed." Nong, our center-forward, scowls. "They've got twelve players so far."

I glance up the field, where the Green team is warming up. We usually have eleven players on each team, so they'll have one substitute and we'll have only ten players.

"At least it's not the Babes in Blue," Alena says. I notice she doesn't call them the Blue Bitches in front of everyone else.

"We can hold our own." The coach appears beside me—she's just finished attaching the nets to the goalposts. "Just get to the ball first and shoot at the net."

No kidding, I think.

I hang with the Screamin' Demons while they take turns shooting at Alena in net. She only stops about half the balls because of her wounded knee and because she's too busy smiling at Daniel on the sidelines, where he's now sitting with Jamarlo and Carmen. Apparently, Carmen knows him, but she knows everyone.

The ref blows the whistle. It's a woman tonight, the one who rants against any jewelry, especially stud earrings.

All the girls head onto the field. I go over to hang with Jamarlo, Carmen and Daniel. Even though I'm not sure where I stand with Jamarlo, it's better than hanging with the coach while she yells useless advice. As the only Screamin' Demon on the sidelines, I don't need the reminder that I'm as useless as our coach.

Under the shade of the trees, Jamarlo and Carmen lean against the chain-link fence with their legs entwined while Daniel sits upright beside Carmen, his eyes on Alena.

They're behind the row of parents, grandparents and younger siblings who line the field, shouting advice. Alena and I have discouraged our parents from coming.

Jamarlo nods curtly as I approach, and I wonder if I've made a mistake.

"Join the party," Carmen says, her fingers hooked into his dreads.

I perch next to Daniel, thinking I can at least make sure he's good enough for Alena.

As the game starts, Jamarlo and Carmen won't stop talking about the anti-prom—apparently, Daniel hasn't heard of it. Their talk is thick with innuendos about how he should ask Alena to go with him. They tell him that it's being held at an underage club, Carmen is one of the organizers, it's for grade elevens, and it only costs ten dollars to get in.

They're practically drooling with excitement, but it seems frivolous. Who cares if there's going to be an alternative-fashion contest? They're ignoring the soccer game in front of them. As I watch the goals pile up against the Screamin' Demons, my guilt grows.

When the anti-prom talk finally dies down, Carmen nods toward my cast. "Joel told me that you punched a Dumpster." She gives me a sideways smile. "Is it true?"

Jamarlo laughs. "I bet it is."

My face heats up. "You know my brother?" I ask Carmen.

"Doesn't everyone?" She giggles in a way that makes me not want to know what she's done with Joel.

Then everyone stares at my cast as if they're contemplating my stupidity, waiting for me to explain or deny it.

"Tori used to go out with Matt Bucknam," Carmen tells Daniel. "From your school?"

Blood rushes to my head. I want to stuff a sweaty soccer sock into Carmen's big mouth.

"You're *that* Tori?" He looks skeptically at my shaved head. "He used to talk about your gorgeous hair."

"It's even more gorgeous now," I say. How do I stop this conversation?

"He still raves about it, even after he broke up with you." Daniel turns back to the game—and Alena.

"*I* broke up with *him*," I snap before I can stop myself. "Matt's a liar!" What other lies is he spreading about me?

Jamarlo gives me a sideways look.

Daniel just keeps watching the game.

"Whoa," Carmen says. "Someone has issues."

I clench my jaw, remembering when I broke up with Matt. It was the week before Carmen's party. Matt and I were watching a B-rated horror flick in the den. He grabbed my phone when it buzzed to see who was texting me.

"Give it back!" I reached for it, tired of him checking up on me, nosing into my life, even telling me what to wear.

Matt pushed me down on the couch. "What are you hiding?" His knee pressed into my groin. His eyes flamed.

"Get the hell off me!" I yelled. Mom and Dad were out, and Joel was in his room with the music cranked.

"You texting other guys?" He yanked my hair backward so that my shoulders arched off the couch. "What else are you doing with them?"

I couldn't speak. Couldn't breathe. Who was this monster?

Then Joel's footsteps sounded in the second-floor hallway. Matt let me up. He apologized like it was nothing. He called it an accident.

I kicked Matt out of my house and my life. After that, I thought I could forget we ever went out.

"Just so you know, Matt might drop by later with his new girl," Daniel says. "She's into soccer too."

"Good to know." I nod. Then, as soon as I can, I make some excuse and bail. I want to avoid Matt and Melody, just step sideways out of my life and escape them, but they keep hounding me.

As I leave, I send Alena a quick text. sorry, I had to go. Somehow, she'll have to understand.

On the way home on the bus, I'm upset about everything that's gone wrong today—Alena ditching me, Jamarlo ignoring me, Carmen gossiping about me with my brother, Matt and Melody threatening to show up.

I find Joel sprawled on the leather couch in the den, watching men's soccer, with a plate of cheese nachos perched on his stomach.

"Why did you do it?" I yell.

His eyes stay on the TV screen. "Do what?" He stuffs three nachos into his mouth at once.

"Tell Carmen that I punched a Dumpster!"

His eyes flick to me and then back to the screen. "You did punch a Dumpster." He sounds puzzled.

"I know! But you don't need to tell people about it!" My brother may be able to solve math equations faster than I can, but his sensitivity skills are at rock bottom.

"Who cares what they know? It's not like you have anything to hide." He turns up the volume.

I leave the den wanting to hit something, but it'll only hurt my good hand. When I head to my bedroom, Mom and Dad cut me off at the stairs.

"What was the yelling about?" Dad crosses his arms and frowns. Beside him, Mom puts a hand on the railing, blocking my way.

"Nothing. Joel is just being an idiot, as usual." I wish he were leaving for university in September so I could have high school to myself.

"You look upset again. What's wrong now?" Mom asks.

"I'm fine." Everything is wrong, but I don't want to talk about it.

Mom and Dad exchange a look.

"I just want to go to my room. I'm tired."

"That's one of the things we're worried about," Mom says.

Dad clears his throat. "Your mother and I want you to slow down a bit. Exams are soon, and you're doing community service every day. It might be too much for you."

"You're the one who made me do community service in the first place, and now you want me to stop?" I shake my head, amazed.

"No." The fine lines around my mother's mouth deepen. "We want you to slow down."

I plant my good hand on my hip. "Well, you can forget it. Casey waits for me to arrive each day. Manny's about to lose a tooth. The others made me promise to play tag with them." I push past my parents. "I'm not going to let any of them down."

As I turn the corner in the upstairs hall, I glimpse Dad putting a hand on Mom's arm.

"Leave her for now," he says.

Damn right. I shut the door to my room and flop backward onto my bed. This time, I won't let my parents tell me what to do.

SEIZE

to take by force

I t's a scorching Friday afternoon, and I'm walking past cozy bungalows to the playground at Mill Pond Park. The bigger kids from the shelter are paired with the younger ones, walking hand in hand, with Jia at the front, Francine at the back and Sal and me midway.

"You have four brothers?" I gape up at Sal. I'm paired with Manny, who's tried to bolt across the street in front of cars twice so far. Once to see a puppy up close and another time to get away from his brother's teasing. His hand is sweaty in mine.

"Yup." Sal slouches along the interlocking-brick sidewalk, hardly lifting his Nikes. "Two older and two younger. Maybe that's why I like kids. We all have to take care of each other since my mother works a lot." He's carrying two-year-old Fatima, who's fallen asleep on his shoulder.

"I only have one brother, and sometimes he makes me doubt the future of the human race." I tighten my grip on Manny's slippery hand as we approach an intersection with overhanging trees.

Sal laughs. "He can't be that bad."

"You don't know my brother." I roll my eyes.

"Sal's mama cut my hair," Manny brags.

I lift Manny's baseball cap, check out his short-cropped black curls and give him a thumbs-up.

Manny beams.

"Your mother did that?" I glance at Sal.

"She's a hairdresser," Sal says, "so she cuts hair at the shelter once a month."

"Wow! Five kids and she still has time to volunteer? That's generous."

"It's nothing." He shrugs, but he's grinning.

Up ahead, Casey checks both ways before she crosses the street with her four-year-old charge from the preschool room.

"I see the park!" Manny's hand slides free of mine and he bolts.

"Manny, stop!" I shriek. I reach with my good hand for the back of his shirt and miss. A large hydro truck is rolling toward the four-way stop in front of us.

Then Sal's long arm stretches out. He grips Manny's shoulder and pulls him back. The truck screeches to a halt.

"Hold up there, soldier." Sal's voice is steady. "Wait for your partner."

He doesn't scream or even lecture Manny. Fatima is still asleep on his shoulder.

"Good reflexes, Sal." I try to keep my voice calm like his.

The truck rumbles through the intersection.

"If you like that, you should see me bowl sometime." Sal's bronze eyes meet mine.

"What?" I grab Manny by the forearm, hoping Sal isn't asking me out.

"Bowling. You and me. After your hand is better."

"Uh, I don't know how to bowl," I say, even though Dad used to take Joel and me regularly. I turn my back to Sal, my chest suddenly constricting so that I can't breathe properly. I can't date Sal. Or anyone. Not right now. Maybe never. "Let's cross together," I tell Manny.

"I'm going on the swings first." Manny leans toward the park, dancing across the intersection on his toes.

"Just stay away from the road," I say.

The playground has four swings shaded by trees, and two adventure sets with multiple slides and overhead bars. In the nearby pond, geese and ducks paddle close to shore, probably hoping the humans will ignore the signs that say not to feed them. The grassy area between the pond and the playground is littered with goose droppings and picnic benches. Beyond the pond is the forest, with walking paths through it to neighbor-hoods with fancy four-bedroom homes and double-car garages.

The kids cut loose as soon as their shoes touch the sand of the playground. I run my fingers over the quarter-inch stubble on my head and veer away from Sal, my chest still tight. The urge to shave again is strong, even though it will be hard to do with my broken right hand.

Rachel gets a game of tag going with some other girls. Jonah pushes Manny on the swing, and I follow Casey, who's peering into a patch of tall grasses near the edge of the pond.

"What are you doing?" I ask.

Casey crouches low to peek under a bush. "I'm looking for Monty," she says.

"Oh." I savor the sound of her voice; she's only been speaking for a few days. "Well, he—and his friends—might be hard to find."

"Why?" She tucks her messy brown hair behind her ears and squints up at me.

"He can travel pretty far. He might be a long way from here."

"Like where?"

"I don't know. How about we look around to see what other creatures we can find? We're bound to find something—maybe a frog or some worms."

"Okay." Casey nods. "But no bees. They scare me."

"No bees. I promise."

Casey spots a purple-and-brown butterfly with yellow-tipped wings, but it flies too high for us to see it up close. I rustle underneath some wide leaves and find a couple of snails.

"Take a look at these," I say. "They have yellow racing stripes."

Casey scrunches up her nose.

"Come on. Snails are cool." I try to remember interesting snail facts. "Did you know their eyes are on the end of those little stalks?" I point to one eye, and the snail retracts it. The other snail is already tucked inside his shell.

"He doesn't like to be poked." Casey frowns.

"Sorry, snail." I bow to him.

"His name isn't Snail." She brings her face closer to him.

He extends his eye stalks, as if he's curious.

"What is it?" I smile.

"I don't know." Casey glances down the path that snakes around the east side of the pond to the forest.

"Can we go see the geese?" She points to two giant Canada geese that are waddling onto the shore, tails dripping water.

"You have to ask Jia."

Casey runs over to Jia, who's sitting on a bench and watching the rest of the kids play. Fatima sits on her knee, blinking sleepily in the sunshine. Sal is at the twirly slide, catching toddlers at the bottom and setting them upright on wobbly legs. I arrive to hear Jia say, "As long as you can see me, Casey. And take Tori with you."

Casey and I walk the path beside the pond, hand in hand, heading toward the forest. We pass a mom with her kid on her hip and the dad pushing an empty stroller. When we near the geese, one starts honking loudly and tossing its head.

Casey covers her ears. "Why is she doing that?"

"I don't know. Maybe to protect her mate?"

"Or she could be asking for food."

"Could be." The surface of the water is coated with feathers, and there are several nests among the nearby shore plants. "My friend came here yesterday to feed bread to the geese, even though you're not supposed to."

"Why can't we feed them?" Casey asks.

"It's not good for them. They need to eat natural food, not human-made things."

"Oh." Her face falls. "My dad used to take me to feed the geese."

Her father. The one who abused her mother and likely Casey too. "Oh," I echo, not sure what to say. I suppose she has some good memories of him as well.

Both geese extend their necks and honk some more. When we don't offer any food, they waddle farther down the path to the edge of the forest, near where other people are walking.

Casey follows them. I glance back at Jia, who I can just see through the scattering of trees.

"That's far enough," I say, catching up to Casey.

The geese stop, and so do we. Casey pulls out some nearby grass and tries to interest the closest goose with it.

I glance toward the forest and notice Mr. Manicure heading along the path toward us. He's swinging his arms and carrying a plastic Wonder Bread bag full of crumbs.

I frown and turn toward the pond, hoping he won't notice me.

"Tori!" He stops beside us, crowding too close. "It looks like we have the same idea today." He grins, showing his perfect white teeth. "Do you want some of my bread?"

"You shouldn't feed the geese," I say, even though I promised myself I wouldn't talk to him. "It's bad for—"

I stop abruptly when I notice that Casey has dropped the grass at her feet and gone rigid. Her chin has retreated into her neck, and the whites of her eyes show as she gapes at Mr. Manicure.

"What's wrong, Casey?" I kneel down.

She's speechless. My creep-o-meter goes off the scale. I glance toward the playground—I can't see Jia anymore—and then up at Mr. Manicure.

His forehead has knotted, and his eyes are filled with malice. "Tell Carita she can go to hell," he practically growls at me before he grabs Casey around her middle and takes off at a run toward the forest.

Casey screams—a piercing wail that jumpstarts me.

"What are you doing? Let her go!" I shriek, sprinting after them.

Casey's sunhat falls off her head. The geese honk. I latch onto the back of Mr. Manicure's shirt with my cast hand, even though it hurts like hell, and land a few punches to his kidneys.

"Jia! Help!" I yell, even though she's probably too far away to hear.

I get in a few more hits. He staggers sideways. I grab Casey's ankle, holding fast. He regains his footing and rips her from me. Then he shakes me off, knocking me backward into the pond.

Casey! I swallow water. Gag. It's freezing. The bottom oozes muck. I thrash around to get my footing, desperate to help her.

My hand gropes the shore. I pull on some weeds to get myself upright.

I gasp for air, coughing and sputtering, wiping my eyes like mad. I kneel. Water streams off me.

"Casey!" I shout, glancing up and down the path. My teeth chatter. My chest thuds.

Casey is nowhere in sight.

FREAK

≥ *to explode with panic* ≥

Seconds pass like hours. I stand at the edge of the pond, rigid.

Call 9-1-1. Tell Jia. Find Casey. My brain fires off thoughts, but my body refuses to react. Inside, I'm screaming, thrashing, punching holes in the sky.

How could this happen?

The sky is a cheerful blue. My clothes are covered in muck and feathers. My shorts drip water down my legs. The Velcro straps on my cast have come loose.

I pick up Casey's sunhat and hold it to my chest.

Jia. Go to her.

I force my feet to move.

My shoes squelch with every step.

Jia. I need her.

I break into a run, desperate to tell her the horrible thing I let happen, desperate for her to fix it.

I slip on wet goose poop and slam backward onto the brick path.

I arrive at the playground smelling like goose crap and pond scum.

My mascara must be smeared down my cheeks.

More than one mother gives me a fearful look, as if I'm the monster, but there are bigger monsters than they can imagine.

My skin feels raw. I stumble toward Jia.

She's watching Jonah swing across the overhead bars. When she sees me, her smile wilts.

"Tori, what happened? Where's Casey?" Her eyes dart to the pond and back to me.

I open my mouth.

Gone, I want to say. *Let me tell you what happened. We need to find her.*

Instead, a wail comes out. I dive at Jia and bury my face in her shoulder.

"Tori, talk to me," she begs.

I can't breathe.

∾

Minutes later, I'm sitting at a picnic table, Casey's sunhat in my lap. The hydro truck is back, parked outside the playground fence. It's lifting a worker in an orange hard hat with the hydraulic arm. How can hydro wires matter right now?

Francine has run down the path to the forest, looking for Casey. Sal has gathered the rest of the kids in a tight knot near the slide. Fatima propels a yellow tractor over a sand mound that the bigger kids are building. Sal watches us anxiously. When he finds out how I let Casey get taken, he won't want to go bowling with me anytime soon.

"The police will be here soon." Jia's face is in mine; straight black hair, freckles across her nose, pleading eyes. "What did he look like? Tori, please focus."

"Um, he's tall. White. Short brown hair. And he's clean." My head spins. The clouds race by. The treetops bend in the wind.

"What do you mean?"

"He's always well dressed. Today he's wearing a collared shirt. White with blue stripes. Pressed pants. Manicured hands." Then I remember the important detail. "He lives across the street from the backyard of the shelter."

"He's a neighbor?" Her forehead wrinkles.

"Yes. The corner house with the blue front door."
I marvel that I can remember such details right now.
"He was mowing the lawn this week."

"Are you sure?" Jia looks puzzled.

I stand up, still holding Casey's hat. "I should have
kicked the back of his knee. It would have made him fall."
I mime a kick. "I thought he was creepy. He…felt wrong.
I should have told you about him."

"Tori, this isn't your fault. But I need you to concentrate.
Tell me everything that happened."

"We can't let him hurt Casey. We have to—"

Just then Francine returns, shaking her head. "I couldn't
find her."

A moan rises from deep inside my chest.

I let the tears come.

❦

I'm repeating my story to two police officers when Peggy
arrives in a rusty four-door. She skids to a stop beside
the squad car and runs across the grass toward us. Rita—
Casey's mom—is with her.

In the playground, the kids from the shelter stare at
us while Francine and Sal try to distract them with sand
toys. I sink lower on the picnic bench and wipe my eyes
with the tissue Jia gave me, but the tears keep falling.

"Tell us everything." Peggy's eyes flash. She grips Rita's elbow as if she's trying to prop her up.

I've let them all down.

Jia sits beside me and holds my hand while I start my story from the beginning again. My soggy tissue is black with mascara. I clench it in my good fist.

One cop writes down everything I say. He's big like Dad, his uniform bulging with muscles. I watch the sunlight hit the fine pale hairs on his arm. The other cop—a small woman overloaded by the gear strapped to her belt—studies me. I avoid looking at Casey's mom. I don't want to see the despair in her eyes.

When I finish, they decide that Jia, Francine and Sal should take the rest of the kids back to the shelter with a police escort. The female cop also radios for a search-and-rescue unit and a patrol car to visit the house with the blue door.

Jia hugs me before they leave. "It's not your fault," she says again, but I know she's wrong.

Sal stays focused on the kids. I'm sure he hates me for what happened. I hate myself for it.

A goose near the pond honks, and I'm instantly mad at it. "If only we hadn't gone to see the geese," I say.

But no one's listening.

Peggy is deep in conversation with the police. Rita's chest heaves with heart-wrenching sobs.

The terrible moment by the pond replays in my mind like a horror movie that won't stop.

"There's one more thing." I sit up. "The man who took Casey—he said something about Carita."

Rita turns to me. Her eyes are red-rimmed. Her tears have gummed up her eye makeup, which is on both eyes this time. "I'm Carita," she says. "Rita for short."

My skin prickles. My broken hand aches. "He said"— I pause, not sure how to say it—"*Tell Carita she can go to hell.*"

Rita gasps like I've slapped her. "It was Stewart. I prayed it wasn't—"

"Who's Stewart?" the female cop asks.

"Her ex-husband." Peggy frowns.

"But he lives across the street from the shelter," I say.

"That's not possible." Peggy shakes her head.

"He must have found us somehow, maybe pretended to be a neighbor." Rita's hands tremble. "He's a good liar. Too good. Oh, Casey-Lynn!" She looks up at the sky, where gray clouds have gathered.

I swallow hard.

"Listen to me, Rita." Peggy's tone is urgent. "Do you have a photo of him on your cell phone?"

"No. I erased them all. I don't want a photo of that man—"

"I can get one." Peggy is on her cell phone in seconds. "Hello, Nathan? I need you to pull Rita Foster's file. Find the photo of her ex-husband, Stewart Foster, scan it, and send it to my phone. Hurry!"

Moments later, Peggy shows me an image of Casey's father on her phone. "Is this him?"

"Yes." I clench my jaw. How could I have let this happen?

Rita rocks back and forth. "Oh no, oh no, oh no, oh no..."

"Try to stay calm." The female cop puts an arm around Rita and slowly lowers her to the picnic bench.

I leap up to give them space.

The cop sits. "We need you to answer a few questions. Can you do that?"

Rita nods. Her chin trembles. Fear lives in her eyes.

"Did your husband—"

"Ex-husband," Peggy pipes up.

"Did your ex-husband ever attempt to abduct Casey-Lynn before?"

"No."

"Has he ever assaulted her or attempted to assault her?"

Rita shakes her head. "He only came after me. I think"—she shudders—"it's me he wants to punish."

"Why would he want to do that?"

Peggy interrupts. "He has a history of domestic abuse, and there's a restraining order against him. He didn't want them to leave him for the shelter."

The male cop nods. "Does he have joint custody of your daughter?"

"No. I was granted full custody of Casey-Lynn last month. His lawyer said he was moving to California. I thought he'd already gone."

I still can't believe he's not a neighbor.

"Will you be putting out an AMBER Alert?" Peggy sets her hands on her hips and sticks out her pointy elbows. "I've heard the first three to five hours after an abduction are the most crucial in recovering a child."

"That's not up to us to decide," the male cop says. "Certain guidelines need to be met for an AMBER Alert—"

"But we'll make a request to initiate one," his partner continues. "And I promise you that we'll do everything we can to get Casey back."

So will I. My eyes well with tears again. I won't stop until she's found.

෴

Fifteen minutes later, police officers are swarming the park. Some investigate the bushes near where Stewart

Foster snatched Casey, and others disappear into the community to widen the search. Meanwhile, police dogs sniff Casey's hat before following her scent into the forest.

I'm glad Rachel, Jonah, Manny and the others are gone, because gawkers are gathering, whispering together and even taking videos of the crime scene from a distance. They're like vultures waiting to pick the flesh off the bones of dead animals—only worse.

From the picnic bench, I can see teenage guys on bikes. I recognize faces, but they're younger than me, so I don't know their names. Some grandmother types with worried faces and gossipy mouths. A few anxious parents. Even a local TV news van with a hungry reporter and cameraman.

The picnic bench is now in full shade. My shorts and T-shirt are clammy against my skin, and I'm shivering. An officer interrogates me again. How many times have I met Stewart Foster? Has he ever phoned me or followed me home? Has Casey ever talked about her father? Do I know any favorite places they went together?

The questioning is endless, but it's nothing compared to what Casey must be enduring. Will he harm her? Will he flee to another country? Is she crying for her mother right now?

The male cop—his name is Constable Wilkinson—approaches me. "We're finished with you for now. Is there someone you can call to pick you up?" He squats down beside me.

"I'm fine on my own." I can't explain to my parents or anyone else what has happened when I can hardly fathom it myself.

Then Peggy appears beside Constable Wilkinson. "You need to go home, Tori. You're probably in shock."

Wilkinson nods. "If no one can pick you up right now, I can have an officer drive you home."

"Good idea," Peggy says.

"No. That's okay." I'm not arriving home in a cop car. I make a show of pulling my phone from my pocket and pressing a button, even though it's waterlogged. To my surprise, the screen lights up.

Wilkinson rises, his knees cracking. "Good. Get yourself home."

"Get some rest. You've been through a lot," Peggy adds.

"I will," I lie.

I don't tell them that I have somewhere else to go first. The corner house with the blue front door. Even though the cops are checking it out, I have to see for myself who really lives there.

I slip away from the police officers and go toward the street. A crowd of bystanders blocks my way.

"What happened?" a middle-aged man asks as I approach. "Did someone drown?"

I push past him. There's an eagerness in his face that disturbs me. People are way too willing to witness the fallout from a crime. But where are they when someone needs help?

I skirt the crowd and head for the sidewalk.

Just as I'm free of them, someone thrusts a microphone in my face.

"Janice Reese reporting for *Glencrest Region News*." Her teeth are bright white, like in a toothpaste commercial. "Can you tell us anything about what happened here today?"

"None of your business." I keep moving.

She matches my pace. "There was a report of an altercation involving a young girl. Can you confirm it?"

I scowl. "Do you listen to police scanners to get your stories? What's wrong with you?"

"The people have a right to know."

I explode in the reporter's face. "The girl has a right to be safe."

She startles, almost dropping her microphone.

"Where were you when she needed help?" I say to everyone gathered around. "If only one of us had been more vigilant, maybe Casey would be safe now."

People in the crowd stare.

I walk away as fast as I can without running.

STAGGER

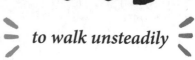

to walk unsteadily

The lawn is perfectly trimmed. Delicate yellow flowers cluster under the locust tree. Terra-cotta tiles line the path to the blue front door.

It's surreal, like nothing bad has happened.

People walking by give me strange looks. They probably think I'm a homeless kid from downtown. I stink. I'm filthy. I sway dangerously on the lawn. I'll probably scare whoever lives here. But I can't turn back now.

I squeeze my eyes shut and wish I'd never heard the name Stewart Foster. If only I could knock on the blue front door and have the nice Mr. Manicure open it. I imagine him telling me his real name—Brad, maybe. Or Kyle. Casey will be playing on the floor, drawing pictures. She'll smile when she sees me. Mr. Manicure will laugh when I tell him about the mix-up at Mill Pond Park. "They think you kidnapped Casey," I'll explain.

I open my eyes.

The front door is wooden, arched, painted forget-me-not blue. A vine is growing around it, clinging to the bricks. As I head up the front walk, the door opens and an elderly woman, maybe seventy, hobbles onto the porch with a purse on one shoulder. She has a boot cast on her foot and a four-pronged walking cane in one hand. When she sees me, a shadow crosses her face.

"Can I help you?" Her eyes linger on my shaved head and my cast.

"Uh, I hope so." I stop at the bottom of the stairs. "It's a long story, but I'm looking for a man I met here a few days ago. It was after dinner. He was mowing your lawn."

"Stewart Foster." She frowns. "Why? Are you friends with him?"

"Not at all." I remember how he ripped Casey from my grasp. "But I'd love to know where he is right now."

"The police were just here asking the same question." She pauses, watching me. "But he's certainly not here. I didn't even know his real name until the police told me."

So it's true. Mr. Manicure isn't a harmless neighbor, no matter how much I wish it. My chest hurts. My head feels woozy. I lean against the stair railing.

"Why are you asking questions about that man?" Her nose wrinkles as she examines me.

"I just saw him…" I grip the railing as a wave of dizziness hits. My knees pick that moment to falter, and in seconds I've crumpled to the ground.

"Oh!" She takes a step toward the top of the stairs and then hesitates. "You just saw him where?"

"At Mill Pond Park." I get to my feet, still unsteady. "He abducted his daughter."

"You were there?" Her eyes widen and then her face softens. "You poor thing!"

Her sudden kindness shocks me. My body trembles.

"What a state you must be in! Sit down." She gestures toward her two verandah chairs. "I'll bring you a cup of tea."

I'm surprised she'd offer tea to a total stranger. "I'm fine," I say, but I feel weak, and my stomach is churning.

"I'll be right back. I'm Lenore, by the way."

A few minutes later I'm seated in a verandah chair, and Lenore is handing me a steaming mug that looks like the barrel of a camera lens. She hobbles back inside and emerges with a mug for herself that's plain blue. The tea smells delicious, and the mug warms my hands.

"Sorry about your cup." She wrinkles her nose again. "My kids gave it to me. I'm an amateur photographer, so they thought it was on theme."

I sip the soothing tea. "It's awesome. Thanks."

She sets her mug down and then gradually lowers herself into the chair beside me.

"It's decaf chai. Won't keep you up tonight." She reaches for her mug. "Now, what do you know about Stewart Foster?"

I sigh, hating the tidy lawn that Stewart Foster has mowed, wondering what's happening to Casey right now and not wanting to think about it at the same time. As I tell Lenore my story, the nightmare images flash through my mind again, and I shudder.

It turns out that Lenore gathered some details about what happened at the park from her conversation with the police. She also knows about the shelter across the street—I suppose it's obvious to the neighbors.

"How do you know Stewart Foster?" I ask.

"A few weeks ago, I ventured into the ravines with my camera for an early-morning walk. I wanted to get some good sunrise shots through the trees, but I stumbled and broke my foot in two places. I got some great pictures of my rescuers, and at least eight weeks in this thing." She taps her boot cast disgustedly. "A few days after I got my cast, this man who called himself Mr. Paul knocked on my door and offered to mow my lawn. I'd never seen him before, but he looked so…"

"Clean?" I suggest.

"Exactly." She turns up her nose. "Maybe he was watching me, trying to find a way to get close to the shelter. But I should have been able to tell he was up to something. Then maybe that little girl would still be with her mother."

"It's not your fault. He's obviously a good liar." I cringe, thinking how he fooled me at first. "Do you know where he lives?"

"No clue. But the police are looking into it."

I set my mug on the window ledge. "Sorry for bothering you, but I guess I was wishing he really was just a friendly neighbor." I stand up to leave, even though I'm still wobbly. "Thanks for the tea."

"You're not going anywhere. We're going to call your family to pick you up here. You've been through so much already. Too much for anyone to handle alone." Her sharp blue eyes meet mine.

If only she knew. "I should be going. I shouldn't have even stopped for tea. Casey is still—"

"Sit down," she orders. "You can't help anyone until you help yourself. I'll get the phone."

∽

Joel's jaw drops when I sway into the kitchen, trailed by Mom and Dad. "What happened to you?" He's got a half-eaten piece of beef jerky in his hand.

"I don't want to talk about it." It was enough to deal with Mom's and Dad's questions and worried looks in the car. I bend over to slip off my shoes, get a head rush and lean against the end of the counter.

Mom grips my arm. "Are you sure you're okay?"

"I told you, I'm fine." I grimace.

Joel takes a step closer to me and inhales. "Whoa! You stink! Did you roll in horse shit?"

"That's enough, Joel," Dad warns, striding around me.

But Joel is like a dog tugging a chew toy. "Or maybe—"

"You don't want to joke about this." Dad grabs Joel by his ear.

Joel yowls. "Hey, cut it out!"

Dad starts walking toward the den. Joel is forced to stumble alongside.

"I didn't do anything!" he yells.

"Let's talk, son," I hear Dad say before he closes the glass doors to the den and I'm left alone in the kitchen with my mother.

I shiver. "Can we call the police? See if there's any news?"

"We need to take care of you first." Mom is all business. "I'll wash your cast the best I can. You hop in the shower."

"But—"

"Don't fight me on this, Tori. You know how worried I've been about you, and now this! I'm going to take care of you whether you like it or not."

I let her tug the Velcro straps on my cast loose one by one.

"Now I know you're upset about Casey," she continues, "but the police are doing everything they can right now, and your job is to wait. You've already told them what you know."

"It's not enough." I hang my head. "This is all my fault."

She lifts my chin and stares fiercely into my eyes. "No, Tori. You're the one who told the authorities what happened! You didn't do this to Casey. Her father did. Do you hear me?"

My chin trembles. "I hear you." But I don't agree.

"I know you care a great deal about Casey, but the best way to help her at the moment is to take care of yourself, so that when she comes back to the shelter, you'll be there to do your job."

"What if she doesn't come back?" My voice rises. "What if they never find her? What if she's—?"

"That kind of thinking doesn't help anyone." Mom lifts my arm and gently pulls off my cast, revealing my pale forearm and hand, caked with grime. "You do stink." Her nose wrinkles. "Joel's right about that."

"Fine." I sigh. "I'll shower. But then I'm calling the police to see if there's any news."

I trudge to the upstairs bathroom. My head feels heavy, and my legs are wobbly. I strip off my clothes, drop them on the floor and prop myself against the wall of the shower.

The warm water flows over me, washing the pond scum down the drain. As my tight muscles ease, my mind replays the events at Mill Pond Park. When I shut my eyes, all I can see is Casey getting snatched by her father, over and over again. I lather, rinse and get out. It's hard to do with one hand, but I manage.

I'm too tired to shave the peach fuzz off my head. In my room, I throw on some sweatpants and an old T-shirt of Dad's that's strangely comforting. I find my cast on my bed. Somehow Mom has washed and even dried it.

The smell of Dad's spaghetti sauce drifts up the stairs, and my stomach growls. How can I be hungry when Casey is missing?

I look up the phone number of the nearest police station. My cell phone only works sporadically, so I plug it in to charge and head downstairs for the home phone in the living room.

"I'm calling to find out about an investigation," I say when a woman answers.

"I'm sorry, but we can't release any information about ongoing investigations," she drones.

"It's about a friend of mine named—"

"To request information about another person, you must supply signed authorization from that individual. You can come down to the station and file a—"

I hang up the phone and march into the kitchen.

"Can you believe the cops won't tell me anything?" I plunk down in a chair at the table, which is set for dinner.

Mom switches on the small TV by the window. "We'll listen to the news while we eat."

"Thanks." I try not to sound surprised. She usually forbids TV during family dinners, and I don't want her to change her mind.

Dad drains the pasta in the sink, and a big cloud of steam billows around his head. "Call your brother. It's almost ready."

∽

I push the pasta around my plate. I'm hungry and nauseated at the same time. The news announcer talks about everything but Casey.

Joel shovels the spaghetti into his mouth and takes a second helping. Mom and Dad quiz us about our upcoming exams, but I can't care about school. Then they go on about how I need to focus on myself, maybe cut back on community service. As if that's the problem.

When a picture of a cop appears on the screen beside the news announcer, I shush everyone.

"Regional police released details of an AMBER Alert today," the announcer says, "after eight-year-old Casey-Lynn Foster was allegedly abducted at Mill Pond Park by her father, Stewart Foster, who does not have custody of the child."

They cut to a video of a police officer giving details of what happened and then a description of Casey and her father and the clothes they wore when last seen. Their photos flash side by side on the screen as the announcer mentions the restraining order against Stewart Foster.

The announcer reappears on the screen. "Police have located the suspect's car on a street near Mill Pond Park, and the quick response of search-and-rescue teams means that the suspect and child may still be in the area. The girl's mother, Carita Foster, gave this impassioned plea for her safe return."

Then there's the annoying reporter Janice Reese with Rita in front of the empty swings at Mill Pond Park.

"Please, Stewart, I just want my daughter back. Whatever may have happened between us, she's not involved." Rita's eyes water, and so do mine. "It's not too late to do the right thing. Please. Bring Casey-Lynn home."

The camera cuts to a close-up of Janice Reese, with the pond behind her. "At 4:30 PM, Mill Pond Park was filled with joggers, kids with their parents and many others, but as one distraught witness points out, no one was able to prevent this abduction from happening."

Then, to my horror, they show a clip of me. "The girl has a right to be safe," I explode onscreen. "Where were you when she needed help?"

Joel cheers. "Good one, Tori."

I swat him to shut him up. How is ranting at a reporter a good thing?

"What was that for?" He rubs his arm.

I sink lower in my chair, ignoring him. I looked more like a maniac than a reliable witness.

"Stop hitting your brother, Tori," Dad says absent-mindedly as he watches the TV.

Janice Reese is still talking. "Friends and neighbors have joined local police officers in the search for Casey-Lynn in the surrounding area. Officers have set up a volunteer base in the parking lot at Mill Pond Park."

I don't wait to hear any more. "I have to help." I stand. "Don't try to stop me."

"You need to eat more," Mom begins.

I scoop a huge forkful of spaghetti into my mouth. "Are you coming or not?" I say through my food.

"Of course we are." Dad pushes back his chair.

Joel gets out his cell phone. "I'll call Roger."

"Fine. But it's against my better judgment." Mom's eyes settle on me. "We should take some flashlights for when it gets dark."

I take the stairs two at a time. When I get to my room, I grab my phone and send out a mass text to my friends, begging them to help with the search. I don't care if I sound dumb or desperate. Only Casey matters now. I hope at least Alena and Jamarlo will come.

When I get a text back, I check my phone.

It's from Matt. My fingers tighten around the phone.

Saw u on tv. Looking good. We should finish what we started.

I throw my phone across the room and head out.

SEEK

to search for an end

My family piles into the SUV, with Mom driving and me stuck in the back beside Joel. Dad turns on the radio, and we hear about the AMBER Alert again. We stop at the 7-Eleven for flashlight batteries, even though it's still light, and Dad reports that the alert is on the lottery terminal screen too. I hope all this attention will be enough to bring Casey back safely.

Joel taps a beat with his fingers against his thigh. I strain against my seat belt to see how fast Mom is going.

"Can you at least go the speed limit?" I grip the back of Dad's seat with my good hand.

"It's not me," Mom says, frowning into the rearview mirror. "It's this traffic."

The cars ahead of us are crawling, even though it's after rush hour and we're on a side street.

"Shouldn't these people be at home watching TV or something?" I scowl.

When we turn the corner onto Mill Street, a line of cars with red brake lights jams the road. More cars are parked in front of the houses, on both sides of the street.

"This is as far as we go." Mom wedges the SUV between two other cars.

"What are all these people doing here?" I grab a flashlight and open my door.

"Maybe they're joining the search," Dad says.

"You think?" I glance at all the people heading toward Mill Pond Park.

As we hike the few blocks to the park, a stream of people joins us, and clouds cover the evening sun just above the treetops. When the playground and pond come into view, I can't help but relive the horrible moments with Stewart Foster and Casey.

I shiver. My broken hand throbs.

Dad grips my good hand as if he understands. Mom squeezes my shoulder.

The parking lot across the street from the playground is packed with people. The two entrances are blocked off by police cruisers with flashing lights. I'd be overwhelmed by the number of people if they weren't all here for Casey.

Red and white lights from the police cars blaze across the faces. I see my World History teacher, Mr. Hadley, with a woman who must be his wife. There's Jamarlo with Carmen and a few other people from school. I spot Alena with both of her parents. Her bald, round father is still in his suit. Her mother gives me a somber wave. Janice Reese blabbers while her cameraman films her and the crowd. Residents and workers from the shelter meet up with Sal and a boy who has to be his brother. They have the same swoop of dark brown hair across their foreheads.

"There's Roger," Joel says, and then he pushes off into the crowd.

"Keep your cell phone on," Dad calls.

"He forgot his flashlight." Mom follows Joel.

Marla, Nong and Trish from the Screamin' Demons swarm me. They look different out of uniform and with their hair down.

"Tori!" Marla yells. "You were awesome on TV. Coach is here too. And Alena."

"I can't believe you came." I shake my head.

"Of course we did." Nong elbows me.

"We're a team." Marla smiles. "Even if you can't play."

They ask me how I know Casey, and I tell them about working at the shelter. I don't mention that it's community service for my supposed crime.

Then I see Lenore from the house with the blue door. She's at the far end of the lot, near a group of six or so police officers wearing fluorescent vests. I catch glimpses of her passing out flyers. Her cane is propped beside her.

With so many people looking for Casey, we have to be able to find her or at least some clue to where she is.

I say goodbye to the Screamin' Demons and make my way over to Alena and her parents.

"Thanks for coming," I say.

"We want to help." Alena's dad kisses both of my cheeks and says something in Greek that I don't understand.

"That poor girl!" Alena's mom clears her throat. "And her mother! That man is a monster."

Alena hugs me. "Are you okay?"

I swallow hard. "Yes. No. I don't know." Alena's sympathetic eyes make me want to collapse against her shoulder, sobbing.

"Were you there…when it happened?" She bites her lip.

Tears well in my eyes, and I wipe them away. "I tried to stop him…"

"Oh, Tori. We'll find her." Alena's eyes gleam, and I'm grateful for my friend. Whatever issues we had seem to be gone. "Come on. You need both your best friends right now. Let's find Jamarlo."

As we're pressing through the bodies toward Jamarlo and Carmen, a cop with a megaphone calls for the crowd to quiet down. I don't recognize any of the officers.

We stop to pay attention, straining to see over the heads and shoulders in front of us.

"Welcome, search-and-rescue volunteers!" the cop bellows through the megaphone. "I'm Constable Riyad from the emergency response unit. We're here to conduct a basic search of the surrounding area, including the park, residential areas and side streets. The main objective is the safe return of Casey-Lynn Foster."

The crowd is quiet now.

"You may have heard that we located the suspect's car on a nearby street, and that we hope the quick response of witnesses and police search-and-rescue teams has prevented the suspect from fleeing the area."

Alena elbows me. "He's talking about you!"

"Yeah, I guess." I shrug.

"We'll be searching the network of nearby parks and ravines in particular, as well as local schoolyards, community centers, shopping centers and so on. Officers are already inquiring door to door in the neighborhood. We have a lot of ground to cover, so we'll be organizing you by task and location," Constable Riyad continues. "But first, a few instructions.

"Do not search alone. Travel in groups of at least two people. Report back here when it gets too dark to see. We don't want anyone lost or injured."

"We'll search together," Alena whispers.

I nod.

"Be on the lookout for articles of clothing or other personal belongings scattered on the ground. If found, do not disturb. Alert a nearby police officer right away.

"And immediately report any sightings of Casey-Lynn or Stewart Foster to the police by calling 9-1-1. Provide information on the location as well as a description of the victim, the suspect and any vehicle involved."

Constable Riyad motions to the row of cops beside him. "Please see one of these coordinating officers to be assigned a task and location. You can also pick up flyers with the photos and descriptions of Casey-Lynn and the suspect." He raises his voice. "Let's bring this child home safe, folks!"

The megaphone squeaks as he powers it off.

The crowd surges forward to the line of officers. Alena and I are heading sideways toward Jamarlo when I bump into Sal.

"Hey, Tori," he says. "I didn't get to talk to you at the park."

Every muscle in my body tenses; I'm sure Sal will blame me for not protecting Casey. "It all happened so fast. I couldn't stop it." I take a step toward Alena, who's still walking. I can't look Sal in the eyes.

Sal pulls me back. "What are you talking about?"

I shake my head and examine my feet.

"You think this is your fault?" He sounds amazed, even angry. "I was there too, Tori. You're not the only one who wishes it didn't happen. Jia and Francine are beating themselves up."

"They are?" I glance up at him.

"Of course they are." His face softens. "We all are."

Then Sal's brother, who looks about thirteen, elbows him. "Oooh, who's this? Your girlfriend?"

"Cut it out, Carlos." Sal messes his brother's hair. "This is my *friend*"—he emphasizes the word—"Tori."

Carlos madly smooths down his ruffled hair and glares at Sal.

"Hey, Carlos." I must have imagined Sal was asking me out when he suggested we go bowling. I'm such an idiot. "Listen, I've got to go. I'm—" I glance toward Alena, Jamarlo and the rest of my crowd.

And I see Matt.

My legs tremble. My head pulses.

"Oh, shit," I mutter. What's he doing here? Did Daniel drag him along? As if Matt cares about a kidnapped girl.

Matt is standing next to Daniel, who's talking to Alena. He's wearing the same bomber jacket he once lent me on a cold evening, and he's brought his golden retriever, Digit. I watch him smooth the fur on Digit's head and laugh with Carmen, who's with Jamarlo. My hands get clammy. Then I see Melody, linking arms with Matt while glaring at me.

I don't want to breathe the same air as Matt. How can my friends even stand near him? How can they fake-smile at Melody? If they knew what happened—

"You all right?" Sal follows my gaze. "Do you know them?"

"Uh, yeah. They're my"—I hesitate—"friends."

Meet my friend Matt, a random guy at the library said to me on a cold day in March.

I was checking out books for a school project that would be due in only two days, so I ignored him.

The guy grinned and shoved his friend forward. Matt's stunning smile and piercing eyes made me drop my library books. Outside, he introduced me to Digit, who greeted him with three happy barks.

I didn't know that Matt would treat his dog better than me.

"Listen," I say to Sal. "Do you want a partner for the search? I could use one." I nod toward Carlos. "Or two."

"Sure." Sal beams.

I silently apologize to Alena as Sal, Carlos and I head over to get our assignment. It's the second time I've ditched her in the last week, but I can't face Matt.

~

The mood at Mill Pond is completely different from earlier that day. As the evening sun dips below the treetops, police dogs in bright-orange vests lead officers along paths and into bushes. Searchers stream to their assigned locations, some by car and others on foot. Sal, Carlos and I head around Mill Pond to where the asphalt ends and the gravel path curves through the forest. We've been assigned a stretch of ravine between two communities of large two-storey homes, and it's a bit of a trek to get there.

In the last of the daylight, we cross a stream that has been diverted into a culvert and pass grasses that are taller than I am. We circle a smaller pond and traverse a well-kept park with a playground. Everywhere, I see hiding places that I want to check, hoping I'll find Casey's scared, dirty face peering out at me. I picture her arms wrapped around my neck as I bring her home to her mother. If only.

When we reach our assigned location, the path disintegrates to nothing. The sun sinks lower in the sky, and the forest darkens.

Carlos wanders ahead, climbing over logs and kicking up the dusty scent of last year's leaves. Sal and I find an old newspaper and what looks like someone's chemistry homework.

The sound of voices and music from the nearby backyards reaches us. A woodpecker taps at a tree, and squirrels go about their business like there's nothing wrong.

When there's a screech from a nearby search team, we rush over. They've found a smashed computer hard drive and monitor, which they plan to show to an officer even though I'm sure it has nothing to do with Casey.

The sun sets behind the trees. We're supposed to go back, but I pull out my flashlight. We find cigarette butts and broken beer bottles. My shoe gets stuck in the mud. As Sal helps me try to pull it loose, he asks why I didn't want to search with my friends.

"There's this guy I don't want to see." It feels strange to talk about Matt. "He's an asshole."

"So why are your friends with him?" Sal is on his knees in the mud, tugging at my shoe.

I put my hand on his slender back to keep my balance. "Maybe they don't know how big an asshole he is."

Sal looks up at me like he knows something I don't. "Maybe you should tell them."

"Maybe I don't want to talk about it." With anyone. Ever.

"Yeah. I get that." Sal gives my shoe another yank. "But do they need to know?"

My shoe comes free with a squelching noise. Sal and I tumble backward together into the dry leaves, my flashlight aimed at the purple sky. I flinch when I land on my broken hand.

"Thanks." When I look up, Sal's face is inches from mine. I gasp. His bangs have fallen over one eye; the other is gazing at me, warm and curious. The freckle on his lower lip is terrifyingly kissable.

I scramble backward, my fingers digging into the earth, pebbles under my nails, a root jamming into the small of my back. As I untangle from him, I'm grateful that his fingers didn't wander to any awkward places.

"Any time." Sal helps me up.

My hand hurts. I rub the small of my back. What just happened?

Then Carlos is beside us, peering into the darkness, his hands out in front of him. "I can't see anything."

I give him a turn with my flashlight and try to stop my hands from trembling. We search for another hour or so, until we finish our assigned area.

When we arrive back at the parking lot, Matt and the others are nowhere in sight, and Mom and Dad are waiting for me. I say goodbye to Sal and Carlos to avoid awkward introductions.

"Where were you?" Mom shines her flashlight on me. "We were phoning you."

I squint into the light. "I left my cell at home."

"Tori, we got it for you so we could stay in touch!"

"I know. Sorry. But it's waterlogged, and I don't think it works." Except to get Matt's text.

Around us the search is winding down, and volunteers are heading home. I don't want to leave without Casey. I march over to Constable Riyad, my muddy shoe squishing with each step.

"What happens next?" I ask him.

The streetlamp shines on his face. "We continue the search at first light," he says.

He sounds positive, but I'm losing hope. All I can think of is Casey's terrified face when she recognized her father. What was she so afraid of?

I head to the suv with my family. It's great that all these people came together tonight, but it hasn't made any difference to Casey.

RiSE

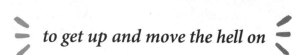

to get up and move the hell on

I wake up sweating. My clock glows in the darkness: 2:16 AM. Nine hours since Casey went missing. An eternity.

A nightmare is still with me. Aliens had embedded a bomb in my chest that was about to blow up the entire world, destroying everyone I knew. The nightmare ended when it detonated.

I throw off the covers and try to stop shaking. Decaf chai or not, I won't be sleeping again tonight.

I get out of bed and go to the window. I can't lie still while Casey is missing. I have to keep going, just put one foot in front of the other. If I stop moving, I might implode, but I won't be taking any aliens with me.

The windows of the houses on my street are dark, the curtains shut. The streetlamps burn circles of light into the grass and asphalt beneath them. Pin-prick stars smolder in the coal-black sky.

Where is Casey now? What will he do with her? I ask the stars, but they have no answers.

Maybe he's pampering her to win her over and make her forget her mother.

But for some reason, I imagine the worst, maybe because Casey seemed so scared of him. I can see her shivering and cold in a damp drainage ditch, calling out for her mother as her father clamps his hand over her mouth. I imagine her in the trunk of a car with duct tape covering her mouth and pinning her arms behind her back while the car hurtles down some distant highway, her father grinning at the wheel. I imagine her tied to a chair in a dusty old cottage, her father standing over her threateningly.

Then I wonder if maybe, just maybe, the police have found Casey while I slept. I open my laptop and check the news online.

No luck. Just an article about the search teams and how the police suspect that Stewart Foster is still in the area. But how could they know that? He could be in another country by now.

I fume at the cops for not finding her and at myself for not stopping Casey's father in the first place. Can none of us help her?

In the corner of my room, I see my cell phone glowing, the message light flashing. I'm tempted to check it, but what if it's Matt?

We should finish what we started, he texted.

I shudder. Does he mean it? Or is he just messing with me?

I hug myself to stop the shaking. Then I head to the bathroom across the hall and dig around in Dad's drawer, keeping the lights switched off.

The straight razor lies beside the electric clippers.

I open the razor, hold it in my injured hand and run the blade along the length of my wrist. Not hard enough to draw blood. Just enough to feel its bite.

My hands get clammy. My chest hurts. Maybe Matt will come after me. Just look at what happened to Casey. Nightmares do come true.

I shove the razor back in the drawer and settle for the electric clippers. In the glow of the streetlamp, I shave my head with my left hand. It's awkward, but I manage.

I staunch the blood from two small cuts. Then I wander through the house, pacing. Dad snores loudly behind my parents' bedroom door. I run my fingertips over the stair railing, the back of the couch, the lamps and tables. It grounds me, connects me to the thrum of the house, solid in the earth.

So why do I feel like I'm spinning?

I find Joel in the kitchen, stuffing his face. He's wearing pajama bottoms, and his scrawny chest is bare. The light from the fridge spills across the tile floor, and cold air wafts toward me.

Mom would scold him for leaving the fridge open. Dad would swat the back of his head. I just shut the fridge with my foot and sit across from him at the table. The light from the streetlamp shines in a swath between us.

"Want some?" Joel isn't whispering, but he's quieter than usual. He nudges his bowl toward me, which is strangely generous for him, and then scoops up a mouthful of Kraft Dinner with a chunk of sugared donut.

"That's just gross, Joel." I turn up my nose.

"Your loss." He grabs another donut from the package beside him. "Shaved your head again? Mom will love it."

I shrug. "Why are you up?" I rest my elbow on the table and prop my head on my good hand.

"Can't sleep." Joel takes another large bite and talks while he chews. "I just keep thinking about that missing kid and the asshole who took her."

"Really?" I wonder what he'd think of Matt, if he knew.

"Yeah. Like, I wonder where the hell the cops were." He waves half a donut around, sprinkling sugar on the table between us. "That reporter said the guy had whacked around his wife before, and maybe his kid, so why was he even out on the streets? They should have had the loser locked up somewhere!"

"I agree, but I can't believe I'm listening to you say it." I shake my head, amazed. "When did you develop a moral code?"

"What the hell, Tori? I'm not some kind of creep!" Joel takes a swipe at my head, but I lean back out of the way.

"Even though you dropped ice cubes down a girl's shirt just to get near her boobs?" I balance my chair on its back legs to avoid his wrath.

"It's not the same thing and you know it!" He gets red in the face.

"Okay, sorry," I say, liking this side of Joel.

He scowls and shovels in the last of his disgusting food. He marches to the sink to dump in his bowl and then digs in the fridge for the glass milk jug, drinking from the spout.

I make a face but say nothing. I won't be pouring milk from that jug for a while.

"Where do you think he's taken her?" Joel finally says.

"No clue." I rub my eyes. "The police think he's nearby."

"Still?" He wipes his mouth and puts the jug back in the fridge.

"Yeah." I scratch at the skin around my cast. "Maybe we should go look for her."

"It's the middle of the night!"

"Yeah, I know." I sigh. "I just wish I could do something."

Joel stares at me for a moment and then asks, "Why do you think he did it?"

"To get back at his ex-wife for leaving him."

"Seriously?" He leans against the side of the stove.

"Yup. That's what she said."

"He's a loser." Joel snorts. "Why not just get a new woman?"

I scowl. "You think there's another woman just waiting to hook up with this guy?"

"Good point." Joel scratches his chest absentmindedly. "His reputation is in the toilet now."

I think about Matt, and how Melody doesn't know what he's like, even though I tried to warn her. "Maybe we need a national database of creeps," I say, only half joking.

"Not a bad idea." Joel nods. "CreepWatch-dot-org. Protect yourself from creeps, stalkers and deadbeats."

I grin—until I remember that Casey is somewhere with her father. I tap my fist on the table, wishing I could save her somehow. "I can't stand waiting, not knowing where she is or if she's safe."

Joel gives me a long look and then strides over. "Come on, sibling." He yanks me by the arm. "I have the perfect distraction."

I'm pulled to my feet before I can object. "What?"

"A *Buffy the Vampire Slayer* marathon. It'll be awesome."

"But I don't want to—"

"Yes, you do."

I let him drag me into the den.

∾

Joel lines up a sequence of *Buffy* episodes and collapses on the couch beside me. Under the blanket Mom crocheted, we watch hours of petite, blond-haired Buffy destroying the monsters that threaten her town. I find it strangely soothing.

Joel digs out a box of Fruit Loops, and I manage to eat a few handfuls. He's a decent brother, at least tonight. When I tell him so, he pretends to punch me in the face and then smiles.

After a few episodes, I put my head on Joel's shoulder, just for a minute.

∾

I wake to someone shaking me.

"What?" I groan and roll over.

Sunlight streams through the windows. I squint, trying to remember why I'm in the den, sprawled on the couch, gripping a cushion like it's a life preserver. Joel is asleep on the floor between the couch and the coffee table, a blanket twisted around his legs.

Dad is leaning over me. He's wearing his boxers and a white T-shirt, and his hair is flattened on one side in a serious case of bed head.

"Didn't you hear the phone?" His voice is urgent. "The police called. They found Casey. You're wanted at the station right away."

HAUNT

to torment continually

I switch radio stations in the SUV, hoping to hear details about Casey on the news, but there's only tinny pop music, a stupid car commercial and boring Saturday-morning programming.

"Did the officer who called you tell you anything else?" I turn to Dad, who gave up the front seat to sit in the back by himself. Joel is still dozing in the den.

"I asked, but he didn't know much." Dad's voice is husky with sleep.

I frown. "I still wonder why the police want to see me."

Mom gives my newly shaved head a disapproving glance, although at least she hasn't harassed me about it yet. "Maybe they want you to identify Stewart Foster in a lineup. Or interview you again." Her hands tighten on the steering wheel. "Whatever it is, we'll find out soon enough."

"I've already identified him. And I told them everything I know." I lean against the headrest and stare out at the blur of buildings we pass.

The radio plays an annoyingly cheerful tune. My mind churns. If only Casey and I hadn't gone to the park that day. If only I had tripped her father or tackled him. I can't shake the feeling that I should have done more to help.

When the news comes on the radio, I shush everyone. Casey makes the top story.

"An AMBER Alert was called off after Casey-Lynn Foster was found early Saturday morning," a female announcer says.

I turn up the volume, desperate for details. Is Casey okay?

"The alert was issued after her father, 39-year-old Stewart Foster, who is separated from her mother, allegedly abducted Casey-Lynn from Mill Pond Park on Friday afternoon. Police report that Casey-Lynn was found in good health and has been returned to her mother. Stewart Foster is being questioned by police. Charges are pending."

"So he hid out in someone's shed?" I'm already trying to imagine what it was like for Casey. Dirty? Cold? Terrifying? "It sounds like he didn't hurt her."

"I hope not, but she's still going to be traumatized." Mom glances at me. "Something like that doesn't leave you."

I avoid Mom's eyes. "I guess not."

"I hope they lock him up for good," Dad mutters. "Men like that aren't fit for society."

"No kidding," I say.

At the station, TV crews and reporters are camped outside the front doors. As Mom parks the SUV, I sink lower in my seat.

"Why are there reporters everywhere I go?"

"You don't have to talk to them." Mom turns off the car.

Dad opens his door. "We won't let them near you."

Outside, I zip up my hoodie and hold my broken hand against my chest. As we head up the walk, Dad takes my right flank while Mom's on my left and slightly in front, like a lopsided battering ram. Even though my parents can be controlling and demanding, I'm glad they're here with me now.

I keep my head down and my eyes on my running shoes.

"Isn't that the witness from the park?" I recognize Janice Reese's voice and cringe.

The reporters, cameras poised, crowd us as we approach.

Then the questions fly. "Are you involved in the case against Stewart Foster?" "Do you know Casey-Lynn or her father?" "Did you injure your hand in an altercation with Stewart Foster?"

I keep my mouth shut and my feet moving while my parents ward off the attack. It takes only a bit of pushing to make it into the lobby of the police station.

I look around nervously before approaching a large bald officer at the information desk. As soon as I say who I am, he ushers us into a nearby room and then abandons us. In the room there's a plain metal table, three plastic chairs and little else. I fiddle with a strap on my cast.

"Is this an interrogation room?" I spin in a circle. There's no two-way mirror, like on TV crime shows.

Mom puts a hand on my shoulder. "It'll be fine."

Dad takes a seat and stretches out his legs. "Of course it will. They probably just want to talk."

I'm pacing when two women enter the room a few minutes later—a tall brown-skinned woman followed by a smaller one with olive skin and dark hair. It surprises me that they're both in regular clothes.

"I'm Constable Nancy Hobbs," the tall woman says briskly, "the designated investigator in this case. You can call me Nancy." She motions to the other woman. "This is Andi Chavez, the children's-aid worker assigned to Casey."

Mom opens her mouth to speak, but I interrupt her.

"How is Casey?" I blurt out.

Mom looks startled. She probably expected to do the talking.

"She's fine physically, other than a few bruises." The woman named Andi has a softer voice. "She's been examined at the hospital. But she's shaken, of course."

"Stewart Foster is in custody," Nancy adds.

"We heard that on the radio." Dad nods grimly, and it hits me like a slap across the face that Stewart Foster could be somewhere in this building. I stare into the hall, shaking. If I met him shackled and shuffling on the way to some cell, I'd want to punch him out.

"Sit down," Nancy tells me. "You're probably wondering why we asked you to come."

No kidding. I perch on the edge of a chair. Nancy sits opposite Dad. Mom hovers nearby. Andi shuts the door and rests against it.

"We were hoping you could help us out." Nancy leans toward me. "You see, we need to interview Casey while the events are fresh in her mind. It'll help us figure out what charges to lay against her father."

"And how to help her," Andi adds.

Nancy nods. "But Casey won't speak. Not to her mother, to me or to any other officer."

"That's terrible. She only started to talk again recently." If Casey isn't speaking again, she must have gone through hell.

"Yes. We understand that you've successfully encouraged Casey to talk in the past," Nancy continues. "Her mother says you have a special connection. It's a little unorthodox, but with your permission"—she glances at both of my parents and then back to me—"we'd like you to try to get Casey talking again."

"Of course I'll help," I say, not waiting for my parents' response.

"Are you sure you can handle it?" Mom asks. "It might be hard to deal with."

"I'm very sure." If she wants to argue this, she'll have a fight on her hands.

A fleeting look passes between my parents.

"Okay," Mom says. "It's up to you."

༄

Nancy and Andi send my parents back to the lobby to wait. Then they lead me to another part of the building.

"We have an idea what happened." Nancy takes large strides down the hall, with Andi and me a step behind. "But we need Casey's statement to build a strong case against her father. If you can encourage her to speak at all, I can ask her a few questions."

"I'll try." I hug my broken hand, dreading Casey's reaction when she sees me. What if she blames me for what happened?

We stop outside a plain metal door.

"Casey is fairly withdrawn now, so don't be discouraged if she won't talk." Andi puts a hand on my shoulder. "I'm sure your presence here will be a comfort to her."

"I hope so." What if Casey doesn't even want to see me?

"Let's go." Nancy opens the door and heads inside.

I'm expecting to find Casey in an interrogation room, but the room is large and bright, with colorful armchairs and a rainforest mural painted on one wall. Casey is sitting on the floor near a coffee table. She's hunched over with her knees up, slowly winding the dirty lace from one of her shoes around one finger. Rita is crouched beside her with her hand on Casey's back. Blank white paper and a box of crayons lie untouched on the table.

"Thanks so much for coming." Rita stands when she sees me. Her hair is in a messy bun, and she looks like she's had no sleep. Tears well in her eyes.

I swallow the lump at the back of my throat.

Casey doesn't look up.

"Your friend Tori has come to see you, Casey." Nancy touches her arm briefly.

Casey shies away. Her face is pale and drained of emotion. My heart aches for her.

Andi takes a seat near the door. Nancy sits closer. I notice a video camera discreetly mounted in one corner of the room.

Rita gives me a pleading look that says, *Go to her.*

I sit on the floor beside Casey.

Casey drops her shoelace and begins tracing the circular pattern on the rug with her finger.

I say the first thing that comes to mind. "I'm sorry for what happened at Mill Pond Park, Casey."

Her finger stops.

"I wish it hadn't happened. I wish I could have done more to help you."

Her finger begins tracing again, this time in a counterclockwise direction.

I pause, not sure what else to say. I feel like I'm battling Stewart Foster for Casey. He's done something to close her down again. How do I open her up?

"Go on," Andi mouths.

Nancy, Andi and Rita watch me, waiting, expecting a miracle.

Casey's eyes are hauntingly vacant. It's like Stewart Foster has snatched her from me again. I'm flooded with guilt.

Nancy clears her throat. "Tori? Are you with us?"

"Maybe this is too much," Andi says.

"I'm fine." I sit straighter. I have to get it together. For Casey.

Casey tucks her knees under her chin and hugs her legs.

"I wonder what the kids at Haven are doing now." My voice is fake-cheery and pitched too high. I try again, lower. "Let's see. It's Saturday. Do you sometimes watch morning cartoons in the TV room on Saturday mornings?"

I pause, leaving time for Casey to respond.

She stares at the rug without blinking.

"I hear that Sheerma makes blueberry pancakes for weekend breakfasts. Have you ever eaten them?"

Silence. Is she even listening?

"I've never had them, but I'd like to. Do you like jam or maple syrup on your pancakes?" I blabber on about my favorite breakfast foods, as if it matters, asking Casey questions every now and then.

Casey is a statue, still and unspeaking. What has Stewart Foster done to her?

Eventually, Nancy motions for me to join her in the hall. Andi comes too.

"I'm sorry," I say as soon as the door closes behind us. "I'm not sure how to reach her." I'm failing Casey and letting everyone else down too.

"Maybe give Casey a few minutes and try again?" Nancy's voice is urgent. She reminds me of my mother in some ways. I bet she's used to getting what she wants, but this time is different.

"That's okay, Tori." Andi directs a look at Nancy. "It was a long shot anyway. Unless you can think of something else to talk about, or an activity that might draw her out?"

Drawing.

I remember seeing the paper and crayons on the table. "There is one thing…" I bite my lip. Could it work?

"What?" Nancy perks up.

"Do you have a ruler?" I ask. "Casey always draws with one."

"I can get one." Andi hurries down the hall. She's back in a few minutes with a clear plastic six-inch ruler.

"Thanks." I grip the ruler. "Let's hope this works."

SPEAK

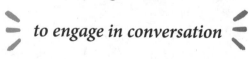

to engage in conversation

I lay out two sheets of paper on the coffee table, side by side.

Casey begins tracing circles on the rug with her finger again.

I open the box of crayons; there are sixteen, and they've never been used. I set the ruler and the purple crayon—her favorite color—beside Casey's paper. Then I pull out the orange and black crayons and begin.

"I thought I saw Monty the other day outside my school." I keep my voice calm and pick up the black crayon with my injured hand. At least I can still draw. "But it wasn't Monty. You know how I know?"

I wait. One beat. Two.

Casey stops tracing circles on the rug. Beside her, Rita shoots me an approving look.

"Because he didn't have a torn wing," I finish.

With the black crayon, I outline the shape of a butterfly with the tip of one wing missing. Casey watches my hand moving across the paper.

It's a start.

I take more than five minutes to fill in the butterfly's abdomen with black. I'm working slowly, deliberately. As I color and chat about butterflies, Casey moves closer. Eventually, she leans over my good arm to see my paper.

I'm thrilled, but I try not to overreact.

"Do you like my picture so far?" I ask, not really expecting an answer.

Casey nods.

A good sign.

I pick up the orange crayon, daring to hope now. "Monty may be small, but he's really strong. He made it all the way here from down south." I pause. "Do you want to draw with me?"

"Yes." Casey's voice is a whisper.

I slowly exhale. "Great." I smile, and it dawns on me that what I'm doing is even better than punching Stewart Foster out. Maybe helping Casey speak about what happened is another way of fighting back.

Casey slides in front of her paper, her leg touching mine. She begins to draw her usual abstract lines with the purple crayon and the ruler.

At first I think she's just drawing lines at odd angles, like I've seen her do so many times. It looks like shattered glass. Then an image begins to emerge. There's a thick tubular shape in the center of the page and wings like stained glass on either side.

"Is that a purple Monty?" I ask. Her picture takes up the whole page.

"Yes," Casey says solemnly.

"Nice," I say. Then I notice Nancy pointing toward herself, like she wants in on the conversation. "Listen, Casey," I add. "There's a police officer here who wants to ask you some questions. Do you think you can talk to her?"

Casey's crayon halts in midair. "Can you stay with me?"

I take my cue from Nancy, who nods. "I can stay," I say. If Casey is so desperate to keep me here, I guess she's not blaming me.

"Okay." Casey continues drawing.

Nancy gives me a subtle thumbs-up. She moves to a chair across from Casey and leans her elbows on her knees. "Casey, I'd like to talk about what happened with your father," she begins. "I know it may be hard, but I need to know what he did when he was alone with you. Can you help me?"

Casey nods. We both keep drawing. I'm adding detail to Monty's wings, inwardly horrified at the thought of what Casey may say.

Nancy begins asking questions. Slowly, Casey explains how her father escaped through the forest with her to a shed in someone's backyard.

"He was mad that he couldn't get to his car," Casey says.

"Why couldn't he get to his car?" Nancy asks.

"There were people in the way."

"Did anyone see you? Maybe someone from the house?"

"No. The shed was far from the house, behind a big bush with purple flowers."

"What did he do in the shed?"

Casey doesn't answer for a few moments. I keep my crayon moving across the page, but I'm hardly seeing what I'm drawing. Casey looks at her mother, and her eyes fill with tears. "He still wanted to get to his car, but he didn't know how. Then it got dark and I got hungry. He made me eat stale crackers and other bad stuff from the recycle bin in the shed. I didn't want to, but he pushed it all in my mouth until I threw up." Her voice breaks.

My stomach clenches.

"Oh, baby." Rita slides closer to Casey and strokes her arm. Then she says to Nancy, "It's something Stewart used to do—force us to eat, especially when we weren't hungry. It was one of his ways of controlling us, and it usually happened before he"—she sucks in her cheeks—"before he hit me."

The orange crayon trembles in my hand. Stewart Foster is one messed-up man.

Nancy nods sympathetically. "Then what happened, Casey?"

Casey adds another line to her picture of Monty. "He said I had to eat bad food because I was a bad girl." Her crayon snaps in two.

"Listen, Casey," Andi interrupts. "You're a very good girl. Smart and brave too. Do you hear me?"

"Yes." Casey's voice cracks. Her eyes are wet.

"I know this is hard, but you're doing an excellent job, Casey." Nancy's voice is gentle. "Can you tell me what happened next?"

Casey picks up one piece of the purple crayon. "He said that soon we were going to a place where it never snows and the sun shines all the time. I asked if Mommy was coming. He said Mommy didn't want to. I started to cry. He got mad." Casey pauses.

"What did he do next?"

Casey presses harder with the crayon. "He yelled and held my throat too tight."

I gag, remembering Matt's arm pushed into my windpipe, silencing my screams. My back pressed against the cold washroom tiles.

"Then he pushed me in a corner and told me to go to sleep. He said he had to find a way to get to the sunny place called Cuba."

"What did you do?" Nancy keeps her voice calm.

"I wanted to stay with Mommy. So I tried to be brave like Tori." Her little hand finds mine, and I hold on tight. "When he got sleepy, I sneaked to the door so that he didn't notice." Casey's voice gets louder. "Then I opened it, but he tried to pull me back inside. I screamed and screamed. He put a hand over my mouth, so I hit him on the nose with my hammerfist, just like Tori showed me. Then I ran until I found some people who called the police."

Casey's body is shaking. Rita wraps her arms around Casey, who still clings to my hand, and they rock slowly.

"That was a very brave thing to do," Nancy says.

Casey clutches her crayon. I nod, grateful that she learned the hammerfist so well, grateful that I taught it to her in the first place.

Nancy asks her a few more questions about when the police arrived. Then she says, "Thank you, Casey. You did a wonderful job of telling us what happened. Would you like to go home with your mother now?"

"Yes." Casey untangles from me. She drops her crayon and picks up her picture of Monty, which is dark with heavy lines. "Are you coming to the shelter soon?" she asks me.

I nod. "I'll be there Monday. I promise."

"Okay." She takes her mother's hand.

"I'll walk you out," Andi says, "and arrange a ride for you, if you want."

Then Casey and her mother are gone.

"You certainly have a way with children." Nancy shakes my hand. "Thank you. I know that wasn't easy."

"Sure." I look down at the picture I drew. At the top, Monty is flying with his torn wing. Casey and I are below him—me with my bald head and injured hand. Casey's mouth is open as if she's singing.

QUAKE

to tremble uncontrollably

Nancy walks me back to the lobby. She explains how I may be called as a witness in Stewart Foster's trial.

"I'll do what I can to help." I concentrate on placing one shoe in front of the other on the polished industrial floor. Casey may think I'm brave, but inside I'm a quivering mess. How can men like Casey's father and Matt exist? Will I ever be rid of them?

In the lobby, my parents are chatting with Rita while Casey hides behind her mother's leg. I'm surprised to see Mom gripping Rita's hand sympathetically.

"I admire your strength," my mother says as I approach. "Your daughter is lucky to have you."

How would Mom know anything about Rita or what she's been through?

Then Mom and Dad notice me, and I'm swarmed.

"Are you okay?" Mom's lips brush my cheek.

"We hear you were a big help." Dad wraps an arm around my shoulder and pulls me in tight.

"I tried." I smile at Casey, who's small next to my father. My legs shake, my arm itches inside my cast, and I feel drained.

"Your daughter is incredible," Rita says. "So generous and determined."

"Yes, she is." Mom gives me a worried look.

I wish this conversation would end.

Rita gestures at the scrum of reporters still waiting outside the main entrance. "Shall we do this?" she asks Andi.

"Sure." Andi nods. "I'll escort you to the car."

"Thanks, although there's something I'd like to say to them." Rita lifts Casey, who buries her face in her mother's neck.

I know how she feels. I don't want to face the reporters either.

The three of them head out.

"Are you ready to go too?" Mom asks.

I nod, watching the reporters advance toward Rita and Casey like a pack of wolves. "Let's get out of here."

Outside, the air is heavy and humid. The reporters have already surrounded Rita, howling their questions.

"How is Casey-Lynn?" "Why did your ex-husband abduct her?" "Will charges be laid against him?" When they see us, the frenzy intensifies, and we can hardly move.

Casey is still hiding her face. Rita steps forward boldly, holding up a hand for silence. I'm amazed when the reporters obey.

"I'd like to publicly thank everyone who searched for my daughter," Rita says. "Police officers, neighbors, friends and complete strangers—you all helped to bring Casey-Lynn home safe. In particular, I'd like to thank Tori Wyatt, whose quick thinking alerted the police to the situation immediately and who has continued to be a great support to Casey and me." Rita clasps my good hand and pulls me into the uncomfortable scrum. "Thank you." She smiles.

I blink into the camera lenses aimed at me, wishing I could disappear.

The reporters bombard me with questions. Do I consider myself a hero? What prompted me to stand up for Casey? Can I describe the events at Mill Pond Park?

I'm speechless. If I'm such a hero, why do I feel so scared inside?

"People are calling you a witness with a conscience." Janice Reese's voice rises above them all. "Would you agree with that assessment?"

I push through the reporters, followed by my parents, and flee to Mom's suv.

~ᵒ

By the time we get home, the lack of sleep is catching up with me. I stagger to bed and stay there for the rest of the day, tossing between the sheets and drifting in and out of consciousness. When I finally emerge, Mom tries to force me to talk about my feelings, Dad repeatedly offers to make me an omelette, and Joel cracks stupid jokes to try and make me laugh. I retreat to my room as soon as I can.

Monday comes, and I have to face my unfinished homework and the last week of classes before exams. There are also messages waiting on my phone, which seems to have dried out, probably because my mother set it in a bowl of rice to draw out the moisture.

Alena sent a text on Friday night during the search: Why r u always taking off on me? Where r u?

I also have a missed call from Jamarlo, which could be good or bad, depending on his mood. And a few happy texts from people who heard that Casey was found or who saw me on TV with Rita.

Who says tv makes people look fat? Alena wrote. U looked great! Call me back already.

It's good to hear from Alena, but mostly I'm glad there's no message from Matt. I exhale slowly, hoping he'll leave me alone.

Then I see a new text from Melody. Skank. He never liked u. No one likes a whore.

Is she a fool? Doesn't she see what a creep he is?

I drop my phone on the floor and stomp on it until the screen cracks. Who needs a phone anyway? I have enough to handle without Melody reminding me of Matt.

I walk to school by myself. At my locker, I notice people watching me and whispering.

"That's her," a girl in grade twelve says. "The one who saved that kid."

"Cool." Her friend examines me as if she's wondering how a puny thing like me could save anyone.

I wish they'd just leave me alone.

I'm jittery as I dump my bag in my locker. I'm missing Jamarlo and Alena—the way we always used to meet up before first class—when they both arrive from opposite directions.

I can't help smiling.

"There's the hero." Jamarlo struts toward me, his brimmed hat low over his eyes and a half grin on his face. "Listen, the Avengers called. They want you to join their team."

"And take your place?" I pretend to punch him.

He pretends to duck.

For a moment, it feels like everything's back to normal.

"Where have you been, Tori? I've been trying to reach you!" Alena hugs me and then kisses both my cheeks.

"Sorry, I was—"

"She forgot about the little people," Jamarlo says, the harsh tone creeping back into his voice, reminding me that things still aren't okay between us. "Her eyes are on bigger fish."

"Like shark?" Alena smirks at him.

"Like your face," Jamarlo teases.

Alena puts her hands on her hips and pretends to be offended. "Are you calling me a fish-face?"

I want to wrap my arms around them both and pull them in for a group hug, but I'm not sure if Jamarlo would tolerate it.

"What's going on?" Carmen strolls toward us, ready to break up our trio.

Alena gives Carmen a friendly smile. Jamarlo dives deep into tongue action with her. I step back. Who needs to watch them slurp out each other's tonsils?

"Well, time for class." I grab my books and shut my locker.

Carmen detaches from Jamarlo. "Hey, Tori," she calls. Her lips are still wet. Gross.

"Hey, Carmen." I tense up, ready for her to say something insulting.

"Good job with that kid." She gives me half a salute. "You're like a real live hero or something."

"Or something," I say. Then I leave for class.

∾

Later that day, on my way into the shelter, Peggy calls me into the office and closes the door.

"Did I do something wrong?" I can't handle more trouble right now.

"Why would you ask that?" Peggy gives me a quizzical look and sits on the edge of her neat-as-a-pin desk. She picks up the phone, presses a few buttons and then says, "Can you ask Rita to come to the office?"

I fidget with the straps on my cast and shift from foot to foot. "What is this about?"

Peggy straightens her shoulders. "I just thought you should know that Rita and Casey will be leaving us soon."

"What?" I gape at her. "Are you kidding?"

"I know you've become quite close to them, and I'm breaking protocol by sharing this news with you, but your situation is unique and we decided—"

There's a quick knock on the door and then Rita steps into the room, shutting the door behind her. Her hair has been dyed three shades lighter, to a golden brown, and it's cut in a tidy bob. I've never seen Rita look so good.

"Did you tell her?" she asks Peggy.

"I was in the process." Peggy presses her lips together.

"She said you're leaving with Casey. Is it true?" I ask Rita, trying not to think about how much I'll miss Casey.

"Unfortunately." Rita's eyes get misty. "Casey and I will be starting a new life. A new apartment in a new town. It's part of a relocation plan the police suggested."

"But it's not fair that you have to leave," I say. "Casey's father is in custody. The police—"

"The police have charged him. There will be a trial, including our video testimony. Stewart will get some jail time. But then what?" Rita shakes her head. "What if he gets out one day? What if he's released on bail? We need to move now, while he can't track us."

I shudder. "Where are you going?"

"I don't know yet," Rita says, "but even if I did, I couldn't talk about it."

"Why not?"

"Rita and Casey have to cut all ties with the people they know, even change their names." Peggy pauses. "They can't leave a trail to follow."

"It's all a little overwhelming"—Rita grips my hand— "and we'll miss friends like you terribly, but it's the right thing to do."

I blink back tears, not sure what to say. That they should stay because I want them to?

"This is all confidential," Peggy says, "but we wanted you to know."

"When are you leaving?" I can't imagine not seeing Casey here at the shelter every shift.

"Tomorrow."

"Oh." I swallow.

"I had to tell you." Rita embraces me and then pulls away to examine my face.

"Does Casey know you're leaving?" I ask.

"Yes." Her eyes are sympathetic. "We thought it would be better if she knew, so she can prepare for it, if possible."

"You can say goodbye to her today." Peggy's voice is gruff. "Just keep it quiet. The other kids don't know."

∽

I leave the office in a daze and wander to the school-age room at the back of the building. The door is open a crack, and I see Casey doing a jigsaw puzzle on the floor with the other kids. Her shoulder-length hair has been styled into a pixie cut. Maybe Sal's mother has been here with her scissors.

I lean against the doorjamb and watch Casey pick up a piece and try to fit it in. It's only been a few weeks since

I met her, but she'll leave a massive hole in my life when she goes. With her around, I feel more focused, stronger.

"What's wrong?" Sal appears in the hallway beside me.

I step backward, keeping a good distance between Sal and me. I don't want any more disturbing moments like in the ravine. "I'm not supposed to talk about it," I say. "Peggy's orders."

"Well, if Peggy's giving orders, we'd all better listen," he jokes, probably to lighten my mood.

"No kidding," I say. Then the tears come, without asking.

Not now, I think. But tears aren't rational.

"Hey, it's okay." Sal's voice cracks. He pats my back with his big hand a few times, and I'm more than a little surprised when I let him. Maybe because he smells good, like oranges. He must have been preparing a snack for the kids.

I lean my head against him and try not to gasp for air when I sob. He holds me tentatively. I only come up to the middle of his chest. His arms could wrap around me twice.

"You okay?" he asks when I get control again.

I have a fleeting thought that I wish we could be more than friends.

"I don't know." I wipe my eyes, being careful not to smudge my makeup, and then ask, "Do you think Casey will be okay?"

Sal pats my back again and retreats a step, like he's trying not to crowd me. "Well, she escaped her father, got interviewed by the police and is still talking."

"She is?" I say.

"Yup." He sweeps his bangs off his face, grinning. "When I arrived today, she told me she has a haircut *like Tori's.*"

"Yeah?" I manage half a smile. Her pixie cut is hardly a shaved head. "Thanks, Sal." My chin trembles.

We lock eyes until a wail from the preschool room breaks the silence.

"You'd better go," I say.

"Yeah. Before there's a meltdown in there."

Then he's gone, even though I wish he wasn't.

I head into the school-age room to share one last afternoon with Casey.

"Great! Tori's here," Jia says when she sees me. "Now we can make those Rice Krispie squares."

The kids cheer, even Casey.

"Sounds good," I say, amazed by how life continues relentlessly no matter what horrible things happen.

We head to the tiny residents' kitchen, beside the main kitchen where Sheerma is making dinner. Rachel tries to take charge of making the Rice Krispie squares, but Jia reins her in. Jonah wants to stir the melting marshmallows "faster than Superman can do it." Manny and Casey can't see into the pot, so they share a chair beside the stove while I stand nearby, making sure no one falls.

At one point, Casey runs her tiny fingers over my head. My hair has a few days of growth; I haven't shaved since late Friday night.

"Are you growing your hair?" she asks.

"Maybe," I say, surprising myself. I didn't know I was considering it.

"Good." She smiles and grips my good arm to keep her balance. "Then we'll look the same."

Casey and I don't say a proper goodbye. I think neither one of us wants to admit it's really going to happen. At the end of my shift, I give her a longer hug than usual.

"Be strong," I say. She smells like warm marshmallows.

"Like you and Monty." Her smile is intense, her eyes fierce.

"Like yourself." I turn away, determined not to cry again. Then I push open the shelter's triple-locked steel door and head home.

FLASH

≥ *to get sudden insight* ≤

Without Casey, the shelter seems smaller. A new mother and her baby move in, and Sal and Francine get busier in the preschool room. I try not to show Rachel, Jonah and Manny how lost I feel without Casey.

But when Rachel yanks me over to admire her painting, I miss Casey's soft fingers curling around mine. When little Manny grins up at me, I miss Casey's huge, unblinking, indigo eyes. When I see Jonah's tight curls, I miss Casey's messy brown hair, so often tangled at the back of her head.

Most of all, I miss how she made me feel. Strong. Capable. Loved.

Life returns to "normal." I watch a Screamin' Demons soccer game without Matt showing up. My parents insist on buying me a new phone, so we can keep in touch. I'm just grateful that I get a new phone number too. No more texts from Melody and Matt. I catch up in my classes and finish my final assignments so I can study for my exams next week. I try to care about schoolwork, but when my mind drifts back to Casey, I miss her all over again.

On Friday, after my shift at the shelter, I head over to Alena's house, hoping she's free. My parents have been hovering over me with anxious faces, and I need a break from their constant attention.

"Victoria!" Alena's mom meets me at the door with their two small pugs wheezing and snorting behind her. "You'll stay for dinner. Yes?" She wipes her hands on her jeans before kissing my cheeks. "I'm making rosemary chicken in phyllo pastry. One of your favorites."

The pugs circle my feet, whining for attention.

"I don't want to be any trouble." I scratch behind their ears, just the way they like it.

"Good. So you'll stay." Wrinkles crowd the corners of her eyes as she smiles.

A buzzer goes off in the kitchen.

"We'll talk later." She squeezes my arm the same way Alena does. "She's in her room." She winks. "She'll be glad to see you."

"Thanks," I say, thinking how much I've missed coming here.

Alena's mom trundles toward the kitchen, followed by the pugs, while I wander down the hall. Alena's house is ranch style, so her room is on the ground floor. As I approach, I hear a top-ten radio station playing and Alena laughing and talking. I hesitate outside the door. Is anyone else in there? Maybe Jamarlo? Certainly not Daniel. Her parents wouldn't allow a potential boyfriend in her room.

Since I can only hear Alena's voice, I decide she's on the phone and push open the door to step inside.

Alena is sitting on her queen-sized canopy bed, painting her nails orange while holding her cell phone against her ear with one shoulder.

"Tori?" She gives me an I-can't-believe-you're-here look and then says into the phone, "I'll call you later, Carmen. Tori just walked in."

I'm not sure whether to feel jealous that she's so friendly with Carmen or happy that she got off the phone for me.

"Sit down." Alena waves to the white, plush chair in front of her mirrored makeup table. "I'll do your nails next. Pick a color." She motions toward her double row of OPI nail polish.

It's a routine we have—Alena doing my nails and me tolerating it. When we were younger, she tried to get me to play dress-up too many times, and nail polish seemed like a good compromise.

I sit in front of the mirror and randomly pick up a bottle of nail polish. It's a hot-pink color called Kiss Me on My Tulips.

"Interesting choice." Alena smirks and paints another nail.

The scent of nail polish becomes too intense. I make a face and drop the bottle. "You should wear it next time you see Daniel." I pick a light mauve. "Sweet Memories?" I read. My memories of Matt are anything but sweet. "These names are terrible."

She finishes her last nail and screws the lid back on the bottle. "I'll find you a good color." She rolls off the bed and stands, wincing when she bends her sore knee.

"Forget it," I say. "I don't need any polish. How's your knee?"

"Luckily, I still need physio appointments. Daniel is a big help." Alena smiles, running her fingers over the bottles and keeping her nails extended to dry. She selects a bright red. "Big Apple Red. It'll be perfect with your pale skin." She examines my cuticles like she's planning my manicure and then runs her fingers over my cast. "How's your hand?"

"Better. The bruises are fading." I hesitate, remembering how upset she was at the hospital. She probably didn't want me to get hurt. It's how I felt about Casey. "I'm sorry," I blurt out.

"For what?" Her perfectly plucked eyebrows rise.

"I don't know." I scan the room like it will help me figure out what to say. A pile of dresses is draped over the end of the bed. High-heeled shoes are scattered across the floor. "I'm sorry for getting violent on Neanderthal, Jordan and anyone else who crossed my path. I know it upset you."

"Yeah, you were out of control."

"I guess." I pause. "And you didn't want me to get hurt?"

"Exactly!" Alena squeezes my good arm. "It's like you had a death wish." Her eyes examine mine. "It scared me."

"Yeah, I was kind of out of it for a while." I don't break eye contact, even though I'm trembling.

"Tell me about it." Alena picks up a nail file. "What you need is a friend right now. Let me do your nails. Then we can talk dresses."

"Dresses?" I lean back against the chair. "For what?"

"The anti-prom." Her smile is a billion watts. "It's only a week away! It'll cheer you up."

I stand up, tripping over shoes as I back toward the door. "I told you, I'm not—"

"Don't start that again." She frowns. "It'll be good for you. Besides, we always go to parties together. Jamarlo says—"

"You can't talk me into it." My throat is tight.

"Why not? Please, Tori," she begs. "You have to come. Daniel is taking me, and I'm nervous about—"

"I can't, Alena. Really. It's not you. Or Daniel. He seems like a nice guy. I just…"

"What?" She sounds hurt.

I take a deep breath. *Tell her the truth.* "I just don't want to see…Matt."

"Matt? Why worry about him?" She doesn't wait for an answer. "It doesn't matter anyway. Carmen says he's not coming."

"How would she know?"

"I don't know. She just knows things. Listen, Matt's no big deal. Forget about him. It's not like he got anywhere with you."

My face falls. I look away.

"I'm right, aren't I?" Alena's voice gets high-pitched. "You said he was pressuring you, trying to control you, so you broke up with him."

"I did, but…" I shake my head ever so slightly. Take another step toward the door. My face heats up.

"He tried to…force me," I whisper. "At Carmen's party. He followed me into the washroom. Locked the door. He got my shirt off. And…other things. Before I got away."

A scene-by-scene playback pounds through my mind before I can stop it. The slick of sweat on Matt's upper lip. His stinking beer breath in my face. His hands pulling me down by my hair, my head slamming against the floor tiles.

Me struggling against the weight of him. His fingers rough on my skin, worming inside my jeans. Music beating in my chest. My screams unheard. Then the press of his arm on my throat, silencing me.

I grind my fists against my eyes, trying to shut it all out. Nothing like this had ever happened to me—until Matt. Nothing like this is ever supposed to happen.

I open my eyes to a look of horror on Alena's face.

"Tori, no!" Her face pales. "Did he…?"

"I kneed him before he could rape me." My body trembles. "But it feels like he did." I remember how I couldn't breathe when he unzipped his fly. Then I aimed, desperate for air.

"God, Tori. Why didn't you tell me?"

I shake my head, unable to talk.

"Did you talk to anyone? Jamarlo? Your parents?"

"No." I grab her wrist. "And you have to promise not to tell anyone."

"Why not?" Alena's forehead wrinkles. "You can't go through this by yourself."

"Why not?" I echo back. "No one came when I screamed."

"Oh, Tori!" She gapes. "I didn't know."

A sob slips from my throat. I let go of her wrist.

"Tell me everything that happened," she whispers. Her arms wrap around me.

I pull away. She holds fast.

Slowly, I give her the play-by-play. How I couldn't break free. How his lips pulled back from his teeth. His cruel fingers, probing inside my shirt, my jeans.

Alena's face goes blotchy. She reaches for the tissue box. I like how she doesn't turn away when I tell her the hard stuff.

Eventually, we end up on the floor, leaning against Alena's bed, side by side, staring at our reflections in the mirrored doors of her closet, me with red-rimmed eyes and her with a tear-stained face.

It's a relief to share the horror, to have someone else know my secret. It makes me think of Casey at the police station, and I get a flash of clarity.

I did more than help Casey talk again. I helped her be *heard*.

When her mom calls us for dinner, Alena embraces me again. She smells like the fruity Body Shop perfume she always wears.

"I still think you should come to the anti-prom, Tori." She squeezes me tighter. "Not for me, but for yourself. You should be with your friends, even if you won't tell them what's going on. Don't let Matt scare you away."

"I don't know." I pull away, feeling like a refugee entering a new country. I'm not sure how the inhabitants speak, what they wear, how they talk. But somehow, I need to get along.

"It could be good for you." Her eyes reflect the sunlight shining through her wide-open windows. "Just think about it?"

"I will." I sigh.

She claps her hands together. "It's a start."

SQUEEZE

to exert pressure on

Late Saturday morning, I'm studying math and munching toast at the kitchen table when the phone rings. I ignore it, hoping Joel will pick it up in the den, until the sixth ring.

"Tori Wyatt?" says a woman. "It's Janice Reese with *Glencrest Region News.* I wonder if you would—"

"No." I start to hang up. How did she get our number?

"Wait, please!" Her voice has a catch in it that makes me hesitate. "I've covered a lot of stories, and something about this one sticks with me."

I lean against the side of the fridge, ready to hang up on her any second. "What do you want?"

"I'd like to do a piece on your version of events at Mill Pond Park. Something about what motivates people to take positive action during a crime rather just than watch events unfold. If you'd just consider talking to me?" She doesn't wait for an answer. "You can call my cell anytime."

She rattles off her number just as the door from the carport opens. Mom pushes into the kitchen, grocery bags in her hands. Dad trails her with more bags. Janice continues yakking. She sounds sincere, but I don't trust her.

"Sorry, but I can't help you." I hang up the phone. Janice Reece reminds me why I'm glad to have a new cell-phone number.

"Who was that?" Mom shoves the bags at me.

"No one important." I take the bags from her and set them beside the fridge, flinching from the weight on my cast.

Dad kicks off his shoes while Mom lines hers up beside the door. As she and Dad unpack groceries, I put my feet up on a chair and concentrate on my next algebra problem.

"It's a good thing you're here," Mom says as she stacks cans in the corner cupboard. "Your father and I have a proposal for you."

Oh no. I keep my eyes on my textbook. "I have a lot of studying—"

"It won't take long, Tori, and it's important."

"So is my math exam."

Dad stops loading the fridge. "Listen to your mother." His voice is gruff.

"Fine." I drop my pencil and stare stonily at them.

"We've been worried about you for a while now, Tori." Mom gestures with a can of tuna.

"I keep telling you that there's nothing wrong. Really. You don't need to worry."

"Now, we all know that's not true. The head shaving? The fights? We've tried to get you to open up, but you're just not talking about whatever's going on."

"Nothing's going on, Mom." I slouch lower.

"So we want you to see a therapist. I've found the perfect one. Maybe when you have someone to talk to—"

"Are you serious?" I straighten up. "I already said I didn't want to."

"We're very serious." Dad crosses his arms.

"Maybe you should stop interfering and let me figure things out on my own." My voice is shrill.

"But you haven't even been seeing your friends," Mom says. "Alena hasn't been around in ages. Jamarlo either. And what happened to that nice boy you were dating?"

I flinch. My cheeks get warm. "I'm going to an anti-prom party with everyone," I say, immediately regretting it. "Is that enough proof that I'm fine?"

Mom sighs. "Tori, just think about it. This therapist is a great fit for you. She's—"

"I have to study." I slam my textbook shut and stack it on my binder. "I'll be in my room."

❧

After my World History exam on Wednesday, the school hallways are quiet. The teachers are randomly patrolling, hushing anyone who speaks above a whisper, and the kids are either writing like mad in some classroom or studying in the library. I'm tired from trying to stay focused on details that don't seem to matter, but I still have two exams tomorrow. My head aches, and my eyes are dry. When I get to my locker, Alena's waiting for me.

"You need to tell Jamarlo about Matt." She leans against the locker beside mine.

I dial my combination, groaning inwardly. "Let it go, Alena."

"Tori, he's one of your best friends. He'd want to know."

"But I don't want to talk about it," I say, trying not to sound harsh. I open my locker and grab my bag. "Besides, he's been…different ever since that day at the mall."

"So? If you explain what's been going on—"

"He's still upset with me, isn't he?" I ask, hoping to change the topic.

"A little, maybe." Alena examines her nails. She hates gossiping about other people, which is one of the reasons I like her.

"Why?" I stare at her nails too. Now they're painted silver, with blue daisies on the thumbs.

Alena's dark eyes flash on mine. "Okay, but I'm only discussing this if you promise to talk to him."

"Fine." I roll my eyes.

She flips her hair over one shoulder and bends closer, like she doesn't want anyone to overhear, even though there's no one in sight. "You humiliated him at the mall with that—"

"Neanderthal?" I suggest.

"Yes, at the dress shop. He needed to deal with it himself."

"But I was trying to help. That guy was a jerk!"

A line appears on her forehead. "Let me put it like this. You're tougher than Jamarlo, and he knows it. You shook his confidence."

I shove my things into my bag, thinking about Jamarlo. "It was such a big deal to him?"

She nods. "He's a joker, not a fighter. You made him feel like your way is better."

"It's not." I shut my locker. "I'm only acting tough."

"I don't know about that," Alena says. "So when are you going to talk to him?"

I wish she'd stop pressuring me. "Soon," I say, just as Principal Hendrick rounds the corner, his tie resting on his bulging stomach.

"You girls aren't supposed to be here." He shoos us toward the exit.

"We were just leaving." I'm glad for the interruption.

As he watches us head to the double doors, we pass the posters for the grade-twelve prom. The theme is "Paris Romance," which makes me want to gag. Of course, there are no posters for the grade-eleven anti-prom: it wouldn't be subversive if it were advertised at school.

"And you're coming to the anti-prom, right?" Alena whispers.

I push open the heavy school door. The outside air is oppressively humid, and my head aches even more. "I told my parents I was going."

"Great!" Alena bounces into the sunshine. "It's going to be a blast. You'll be happy you went."

My stomach compresses into a tight ball. "I hope so." I plod after her, squinting.

∽

At the shelter later that day, the kids paint cutouts of a paper tree to assemble on the wall. It's part of Jia's make-our-own-garden project. Jonah happily paints the trunk with layers of black, gray and blue—the colors of Batman's cape, according to him. Rachel has painted most of the leaves in shades of green, with Manny's help, and is now painting red and yellow flowers. Manny tugs on the bottom of my shorts, leaving a splotch of paint behind.

"Can you draw me the shape of a butterfly?" His voice is solemn. "Casey would want Monty to be in our garden."

"Sure, Manny." I smile sadly, missing her still. "She'd like that."

I draw the outline of a butterfly for Manny and then one for me. He paints his butterfly rainbow colors. Mine is decorated with straight, purple lines.

When Rachel sees our butterflies, she makes one too. Even Jonah does, a gray-and-black one that looks somewhat like a bat.

Jia tapes the cutouts to the wall as soon as they're not dripping. "It's beautiful!" she exclaims when the wall garden is filled with butterflies.

Rachel nods. "Casey would be happy."

"She'd love it," I say. I'm amazed that, after all they've been through, these kids radiate such kindness.

"I miss her." Manny grips my hand.

"We all do, stupid." Jonah whacks his brother, but not hard enough to earn a time-out from Jia.

"Where do you think Casey is?" Rachel asks.

It's the same thing I've been wondering. What town are they in? Have they found an apartment? Has she made friends at school? What is she doing right now?

"Who knows?" Jia grips her shoulder. "But wherever she is, I'm sure she thinks about you too."

As Jia begins Homework Club, I take the brushes to the washroom in the hall to clean up. When I look in the mirror, I'm surprised how gray I look, with big circles under my eyes and smudged mascara. My hair has grown to almost half an inch. My cast has paint on it. I don't look tough, just sad and unkempt. Too pathetic for anti-prom.

My stomach squeezes tighter. Should I shave my head for anti-prom? I can hardly style it when it's so short. What should I wear? I have to look tough enough to survive anything that might come at me.

I finish washing the brushes and step into the hall, tumbling into Sal, who's carrying a cardboard box of picture books.

"Whoa, sorry." He swerves around me. "New dona-tions." He rattles the box, grinning. "I guess it's story time."

I step backward and try to sound cheerful. "Sounds good."

His grin fades. "What's wrong?"

"Nothing. Why?"

"Are you sure? Because you usually clench your jaw like that when you're upset."

"I do?"

"Yeah." Sal puts down the box and leans against the wall. "So what is it? I mean, if you want to talk."

"Well," I say, "I'm upset about this party I've promised to go to, even though I'd rather avoid it. It's just going to be…" I trail off, surprised that I'm so comfortable spilling my guts to Sal.

"Does this have anything to do with that guy you've been avoiding?"

"A bit." I stare at him. He remembers that?

"Well, you don't have to go, but if you do, make sure you've got some good friends there to help."

Like you, I think. But I don't dare ask him to come with me. I mean, I'd like him there, as a friend, but asking him is too scary, too complicated.

"I will," I say, and then I duck into the school-age room for the end of Homework Club.

After my shift, I hurry home, heading straight for the upstairs bathroom and Dad's electric clippers.

I start on my left side. Since I'm using my left hand, I'm a bit sloppy, leaving a shaved patch shaped like a Nike swoosh above my ear. I'm about to shave a second strip when I get an idea.

Using the edge of the clippers, I widen the swoosh into a stylized wing.

Not bad, I think.

I shave the rest of my head down to quarter-inch stubble and then attempt to carve a matching wing on the right side. When I get the wings mostly even, I stand back and take a look.

My stubble sparkles blond in the overhead light. I have to turn sideways to see my wings. One is larger than the other and lopsided.

I practice my don't-mess-with-me glare in the mirror.

Maybe I can be as strong as Casey thinks I am.

CLENCH

to hold tight

Sensation Alley sounds more like a strip bar than an underage club.

There are six steps up to the club; it's in a row of shops on High Street where a mega video store used to be. Alena is tottering up the last few steps in four-inch heels, with Daniel and me gripping her on either side. She's happily missing the point of an anti-prom in a poufy yellow dress that would suit Belle from *Beauty and the Beast*.

When I arrived at her place earlier, she said, "I was trying to decide between a beaded, pink strapless and a purple, one-shoulder maxi until I found this beauty at Value Village—only twenty bucks!" She twirled, making the crinoline underskirt flare out.

"What a deal." I'd tried to sound supportive as she towered over me in her heels.

Daniel is wearing a T-shirt from Tiny Tom's Donuts with jeans and a patient expression. Once again, I think he may be good enough for Alena.

I considered dressing in army gear to look tough, or a nondescript black dress to blend in. In the end, I chose both tough and camouflage: a belted burgundy minidress with a black spider-web pattern and long sleeves that partly cover my cast, and pointy black flats with a nonslip tread—good for kicking or fleeing.

We're fashionably late, thanks to Alena's bad directions, and the party sounds like it's well under way. The bass from the dance music thuds in my chest, reminding me of the blaring tunes at Carmen's party. I hesitate on the last step, clutching the railing and scanning the room for Matt, until Alena yanks me through the doorway and past a thug in a black T-shirt labeled *Security*.

We walk under a banner announcing the anti-prom and into the crowd. The place reeks of cologne with an undercurrent of sweat. The walls are mirrored, and the floor is black tile. The purple lights are dim enough for people to act like fools on the dance floor, and a mirror ball makes the room feel like it's spinning unpleasantly.

On one side of the room, there's a guy serving drinks from behind a bar and a refreshment table piled with platters of snacks. No booze, of course, although the smell is in the air, so it's been smuggled in somehow.

On the other side, a hired DJ blasts tunes from a raised platform that could also house a band. One corner of the room is cordoned off with a rope so people can pose for a photo in front of a backdrop of King Kong on the Empire State Building. I don't know what Carmen and the other planners were thinking.

"Let's find Jamarlo," Alena shouts into my ear. Then she's towing Daniel and me through the crowd on the dance floor.

Alena's dress is the fanciest by far, and there are no rented tuxes. I grip her arm as she pulls me past guys in funky shirts grooving with fashionistas in tight, low-cut dresses and even black leather outfits. I see a guy from my math class wearing jeans and a snowboarding hat. A few girls are in casual American Eagle gear; another is in a hijab.

The crowd is wired on sugar, loud tunes and whatever else. I hold my broken hand close, wishing I'd asked Sal to come.

Then I spot Jamarlo, and I can't help but gape. He's wearing the red, strapless dress I teased him about trying on in Felipe's Glam Boutique, with Doc Martens and his trademark fedora—a black one—over his stumpy dreads.

"Shit! Look at Jamarlo!" I yell over the music.

Jamarlo struts toward the stage, waving at everyone. The crowd parts for him, and he's so outlandish that people laugh and smile. It's strange, but he looks more masculine, and more confident, in this dress. As he leaps up the two steps onto the stage, Carmen joins him. She's in a sequined white tux with tails, accented with a jeweled cane, white short shorts and knee-high white boots. Her bleached-blond hair and her whole outfit glow purple in the lights.

Together, they're stunning.

Carmen signals the DJ, who turns the music down.

Jamarlo whips the mic off its stand. "Hey, grade elevens! Guess who's your MC for the night?" He sets his hat low over his face and moonwalks across the stage; he's been practicing that move for eons.

The room explodes with cheers, yelps and hoots. Jamarlo bows and then attempts to curtsy.

"I can't believe him!" I shout to Alena and Daniel.

"He's gorgeous!" Alena shrieks. "Would you do that?" she asks Daniel.

"No way." He shakes his head and watches Jamarlo with something like admiration.

"First order of business is to thank the organizers"— Jamarlo motions toward Carmen with a flourish—"the supreme party queen Carmen Carter and her team!"

Carmen gives a Queen Elizabeth wave, and the crowd goes wild. As Jamarlo tips the mic toward her, she lays an arm across his shoulders.

"Who says we have to wait till high school is over to celebrate?" She fist-pumps the air. "Let's party!" She gives Jamarlo a long kiss on the lips.

The crowd hoots again.

After the kiss, Jamarlo's grin is huge. "So we've got DJ Malcolm Mix taking your song requests, and a photo booth to capture your memories with King Kong. Also, anyone who wants to be in the alternative-fashion contest, head to the stage in fifteen minutes. Party on!" He swings the mic back in its stand and slides off the stage with his arm around Carmen.

"Carmen knows cool," Alena yells at me as the music resumes full volume. "Or maybe she just makes things cool."

I nod. "Like Jamarlo."

"No kidding!" She beams. "Let's go find him."

"I'll get us some drinks." Daniel heads to the bar, after he gives Alena a peck on the cheek that makes her flush.

We have to fight our way to Jamarlo and Carmen, who've been swarmed. By the time we get close, Daniel has returned, cradling three glasses of soda.

"Thanks," I shout, taking one as Alena snuggles against him with her drink.

When Jamarlo finally sees us, he dives through the throng.

"You like?" He strikes a pose, tipping his hat.

"God, yes!" Alena hugs him.

"You've got guts." Daniel fist-bumps him.

Jamarlo's eyes land on mine and hesitate.

"Look," I call over the music. "About that guy at Felipe's. I'm sorr—"

"Forget about it." His eyes slip to Alena and then back to me. "I get it."

"You do?" That was easy. I wonder why until I notice Alena's guilty expression.

"You told him?" I turn on her, ready to unleash my inner demons on her head, but I'm suddenly relieved that Jamarlo knows about Matt and that I don't need to say it out loud again.

"Told him what?" Daniel and Carmen say at the same time and then look at each other in surprise.

"Nothing much," Alena says. "Jamarlo and Tori just had to work out this thing."

"Cool." Carmen nods. Then, before I can stop her, she's rubbing her hand over my shaved head, fingering the wing designs. "Nice hair."

"Uh…thanks."

She's the first one who has commented. Even Alena and Jamarlo haven't said anything yet.

"This party is awesome, Carmen," Alena gushes.

"Yup." Carmen reaches into her shirt to adjust her bra strap. "High school is crap, but there are perks."

I smile. It's as close as Carmen can get to sentimental.

As we chat about her King Kong inspiration, a good feeling washes over me. The world can be amazingly bleak and harsh, but this party has a random togetherness that feels okay.

When Jamarlo and Carmen leave to organize the fashion contest, Alena begs me to go to the washroom with her. She walks one step ahead of me, raving about Daniel as we weave our way toward it. I bump into Joel, still in his rented tux but without his prom date.

"Why aren't you at prom?" I say, losing track of Alena. Only a few hours ago, Dad was taking photos of Joel and his date, a grade-eleven fangirl, in the front garden.

"I knew this would be better." He eyes a nearby girl in a dress that barely covers her important bits.

"It's for grade elevens only." I'm suddenly protective of this party and even the people at it.

"Relax, Tori. Carmen will bend the rules for me. It's not like I'm graduating." He fishes an ice cube out of his drink.

I frown. "Joel, if you shove that down any girl's—"

"Trust me. I won't make a scene." Still holding the ice cube, he plucks the flower from his lapel and tucks it behind my ear. "Don't do anything I wouldn't do, sibling." He winks and then disappears into the crowd.

I shake my head and aim for the washroom, looking for Alena. Onstage, Jamarlo has the mic again, and he's talking about how we'll vote on outfits by applause. Personally, I think he should win the fashion contest.

The washrooms are behind the stage, down a long corridor near the back door. On the washroom doors are signs that say this is an LGBTQ event, so the washrooms are gender neutral. I bet this was Carmen's idea. I'm gaining a new respect for her.

I push open the door, holding my breath at the scent of crap and perfume. Alena's not inside. Maybe the stink overwhelmed her. I peek under the stall doors for her high heels. No luck. The washroom is emptying out—maybe because of the fashion contest.

Then a loud thud from the last stall gets my pulse racing. A girl squeals like she's in pain.

"Stop it!" Her voice is urgent.

I recognize the voice but can't place it.

There's another, harder thud, and my good hand forms a fist.

"What's going on?" My voice wavers.

I'm stepping toward the stall, not sure what I'm going to do, when the door bursts open and Matt tumbles onto the floor—on top of Melody.

Her dress is open, and his hand is on her neck. His white dress shirt is unbuttoned and untucked. They reek of booze.

"Get off her!" I screech, and dive at him. Melody's been a bitch to me, but I can't watch him hurt her.

I rip his hand off her neck and pummel his head with the side of my cast, not caring about the pain coursing up my arm. My cell phone falls from my pocket and gets kicked into a stall.

"What the hell, Tori?" Matt lashes out, knocking me to my knees near the row of sinks before he leaps to his feet. His face is red, and there's a scratch on one cheek. "I knew you were jealous, but this is insane!"

Melody tugs her dress closed. Her face is pale. Her eyes avoid mine as she flees the washroom, tottering on high heels.

I rise slowly, body tense, not daring to glance away from Matt. The fluorescent light by the door flickers. Outside, the crowd hollers. In the stall behind Matt, my phone vibrates.

"You'll pay for this, Tori." Matt rubs his head, scowling, but his eyes travel my body like he's assessing every bit of it.

My lungs empty of air. I know that look.

I sprint for the door with Matt right behind me. When I push it open, he grabs for me, hooking his fingers under my belt. I claw at him until I'm free, ending up in the hall by the back door with Matt blocking the way to the club. Beyond him, I can hear Jamarlo's voice over the mic, followed by loud cheers.

"You shouldn't mess with me, Tori." Matt saunters closer, his face in shadows.

The scent of his cologne sickens me. I scramble backward, banging my cast arm hard against the wall and reaching for the knob to the back door with my good hand. When I get the door open, I burst into the unlit lane and run.

The night air is cold. My eyes take precious seconds to adjust to the darkness. I crunch over broken glass and splash through a puddle near a pile of crates.

When I reach a main street, I'm breathing hard, my sides aching. I lean against the window of a vacuum-repair shop to catch my breath. What have I done? Will he come after me?

Then I hear footsteps coming from the lane.

I flatten against the glass, wishing I could melt into the shop.

Matt steps into the light, his shadow lengthening on the sidewalk.

My limbs stiffen. He glances around and sees me.

I take off down the street.

"Get back here, Tori!" He pounds after me.

EXPLODE

*to be forcibly propelled in multiple
directions at the same time*

My arms pump. My lungs burn.

I race past several people and one, two, three darkened storefronts, faster than I've ever run.

Matt's feet batter the pavement behind me.

I veer around recycling bins, between parked cars and onto the road. I can never run fast enough or far enough. I'll never be free of him.

My head spins. I want to throw up.

I stumble and fall, bracing for impact, ready to fight until my breath fades.

Matt plows into me. I land a feeble punch. He grabs my shoulders and shakes until my head is Jell-O.

"You think you can hit me and get away with it?" he roars.

I used to wonder the same thing.

The lights from a coin laundromat brighten the street. A tiny man limps out, gawking.

"Go away, old man," Matt snarls, and the man scurries inside, still staring uselessly.

Words have left me. I hang in Matt's grip and aim a kick at his shin, but he blocks me. He drags me toward a narrow alley beside the laundromat.

"You need to learn who's in charge," he says.

My leg scrapes painfully against a car bumper. A car travels past, headlights abandoning me.

The alley is a dead end. It smells like piss and rot. Matt drops me beside a Dumpster.

"Now we can be alone." He knees me in the gut twice. "It's what you wanted, wasn't it?"

I take in the pain, let it sit in my gut, wrap around my neck, eat away at my soul. Then I kick back, aiming for his ankle, as if it will matter.

Matt steps aside, his laughter dark and cruel. "That's what I like about you, Tori. You never give up." He punches my left eye, and I can feel it start to swell. Then he pulls me up and presses me against the brick wall of the laundromat, crushing his hard body into mine.

I squirm, but he has me pinned. His fingers push up my dress, find my thigh. His boozy breath fills my lungs. I close my right eye—the left one is swollen shut now— and try not to feel.

A noise grows in the street. Voices.

I strain to hear. Matt doesn't seem to notice. He's too busy grinding against me.

"Tori!" a girl calls.

My eyes pop open. Alena?

Pressure builds inside my skull. A crowd of voices echoes off the buildings, ringing between my ears, banishing the silence.

They've come for me? It sounds like half the party is clomping into the street. Did Melody tell them about Matt? Did Alena? I stare at the graffiti on the opposite wall, feeling almost human again. There, in the purple letters of someone's tag, I see hard, straight lines like in Casey's drawings.

The pain—in my left eye, in my broken hand, in my scraped leg—bursts to life. The bricks dig into my back. Matt's fingers probe my body. The stench of his cologne infects my pores. The pressure in my head, my chest, my gut, intensifies.

I lean into Matt and chomp down hard on his earlobe, tasting blood. It's not much, but it makes him jerk back far enough that I can get my knee free.

I bring it up hard where it counts.

He blocks it. "Not this time, Tori." He grins.

I stomp on the bridge of his foot and then aim again.

My knee sinks deep.

"Shit!" He hits the ground and rolls in the filth at my feet, moaning and clutching himself.

I shake uncontrollably.

Melody is the first to reach the alley. Then Alena, in bare feet, holding her crinoline up out of the grime. Jamarlo in his goddamn dress. Carmen, swinging her jeweled cane like she's out for a stroll. Daniel, gaping. Joel, pale as stone.

More people gather, some recording with camera phones, others snapping shots, witnessing the truth.

My body aches. My eye throbs.

I find my voice.

"He tried to rape me." The words flutter free. "Again."

The silence hangs for two beats. Then everyone reacts at once.

Melody steps toward Matt, leans down and slaps him hard across the face.

Carmen gasps.

Joel puffs out his chest like Dad does. "Let me at him!"

I block Joel. "No. We should call the police."

Daniel is at Joel's side, fingers clenched into fists. He glares at Matt. "What's wrong with you?"

"She's lying." Matt can barely talk. I landed a solid one.

"Did she give herself a black eye?" Joel draws back his fist.

"I said *leave it*." I glare until Joel backs off.

"I can call." Alena drops her skirts to find her phone.

"Ask for Constable Nancy Hobbs," I say.

"I already called." Jamarlo stands with us.

"So did I," a dozen people echo.

I nod. I'm in too much pain to smile.

Matt rises to his knees, his white dress shirt streaked with dirt.

"Where do you think you're going?" Joel glowers.

Police sirens blare, coming closer. Matt's eyes are like a trapped animal's. He lurches to his feet, wincing.

"Don't let him get away!" says a guy I've never talked to in three years of high school.

"Take him down!" yells a girl I don't even know.

"The police will get him," I say, overwhelmed. I don't want anyone else hurt.

Matt's face is gray. His panicked eyes dart toward me and then away. He heaves himself straight at the crowd, but they refuse to let him pass.

"You're not going anywhere, dumbass," Joel says.

Then Daniel grabs Matt from behind, pinning his arms behind his back in a submission hold. The crowd yells at Matt. A few people head to the end of the alley to watch for the police.

I watch Matt squirm. Pathetic. Clumsy. Terrified. Why did I think that speaking out would hurt me?

I sag, suddenly exhausted. Alena and Jamarlo prop me up.

"Are you okay?" Alena sounds anxious.

I shake my head, not sure how to answer. Why did I ever doubt her friendship?

"If I'd known"—Carmen brings her face close to mine, her lip curled up—"I would have castrated him." She grasps my good hand with both of hers.

I hold on tight. "Thanks."

Police lights flash red and white in the street. I notice Melody slumped against the brick wall. Her tear-filled eyes meet mine.

I've never seen the terror of the soccer field vulnerable.

I break from Alena and Jamarlo to make my way over to her just as she takes off down the alley. Her shoulders are hunched. She holds her sides.

"Melody," I call. "We can talk to the police together. We can tell them about Matt."

Melody keeps going without breaking her stride.

MEND

to patch up

Courage isn't just about being brave for someone else; it's being brave with someone else.

Six weeks after the anti-prom, I'm at Cosmic Bowling Alley with Alena, Carmen, Jamarlo and Sal. After Matt first tried to rape me, I pulled away from my family and friends. Now I'm patching my relationships back together with tape, glue, spit or anything else that might work. It's taken me too long to realize that I need others to help me witness the truth and speak out about it.

The overhead lights buzz, and bowling balls clink together as they roll into place on the ramps. Sal sits next to me on a two-seater bench, his legs stretched out into the aisle. As Alena picks up a bowling ball, she wiggles her eyebrows at us.

I roll my eyes.

Sal just laughs.

"Watch this awesome technique." Alena squats to swing the bowling ball between her legs with both hands before releasing it into the gutter.

We all applaud.

"I told you I need gutter guards." She leans against my shoulder to watch the ball travel the lane without hitting anything. She's hardly left my side since the anti-prom, which is why she and Daniel are taking a break. *I'm fine*, she told me after he suggested it, even though I begged her to work it out with him. *I have my friends.* Maybe their relationship was too new to survive that much time apart. Maybe Alena got tired of hearing about Matt from Daniel's friends, some of whom still hung out with him.

Matt can suck the romance out of any relationship.

"No way are we using fricking gutter guards." Carmen executes a perfect release with her custom bowling ball and personalized sure-grip shoes. I never would've guessed she'd been in a bowling league. "You just need to master your stance," she tells Alena.

"And your grip," Sal adds.

"Good luck teaching her." Jamarlo grins.

Alena pretends to swat him.

When Carmen gets another strike, Alena says, "You need to show me how to do that."

"Try this technique," Jamarlo announces.

We all laugh when he positions himself backward in the lane, fedora cut low over his eyes. With one hand, he releases a beautiful shot—if it could talk, it would be singing—and all ten pins clatter and fall.

"Did you see that?" Jamarlo struts back to where we're sitting.

Alena and Sal give him a high five.

"Way to go, Jamarlo," I say.

"You're awesome, babe." Carmen kisses him.

Jamarlo has been spending more time with me too. I'm grateful for his sense of humor. Carmen comes as well, since they're rarely separated, but I've changed my mind about her. She may be blunt, but she's honest. And she's quirky enough to like Jamarlo, which has to count for something.

Sal slouches up to retrieve a bowling ball. Since he invited me and my friends to Cosmic Bowling in the first place, I expected him to be a shark. But he's nonchalant as his arms and legs lengthen and contort before he flings the ball down the lane and topples three of the ten pins.

He grins at me, and I can't help but return it. I wish I could be that casual, that content. Sal has never pushed me to be more than friends; he accepts what we are when I don't even understand it yet.

Sal finishes his turn, leaving five pins standing. As I head up to choose a bowling ball, his hand brushes my arm and I don't even flinch.

A lot has happened in the weeks since the anti-prom. I told my story to Constable Nancy Hobbs, who interviewed Melody as well. Matt was arrested and then released on bail with a restraining order forbidding him to come near either of us. He hasn't disobeyed my order yet, although I'm still jittery when I go out. Since he's not a young offender, there's no media ban, and Janice Reese is on his trail. I don't envy him that. After the media story broke, another girl came forward with a similar tale about Matt. I wasn't surprised.

At the hospital, I found out that the old man at the laundromat was first to call the police. People can surprise you. Like Joel, who never left my bedside in the emergency room, even for food.

Dr. Balestra said I hadn't rebroken my right hand, although it did swell badly. Now the cast is off and my black eye is gone, but I doubt the bruises on my insides will ever fade completely.

My parents insisted on therapy, which isn't so bad. Some memories of Matt still get me shaking. My therapist says that if I can write my story, deal with what happened, Matt and Stewart Foster will become part of my survivor experience. Like other memories, they may become less important, even if new triggers remind me of them.

I hope it's true.

As I pick up my bowling ball, I catch a glimpse of a little girl with sandy-brown hair flinging a ball down a neighboring lane.

I do a double take, sure it must be Casey. It's not the first time. I see her at the mall, walking down the street, in the school parking lot, at the shelter. She's everywhere all the time, with me in my thoughts, but never in person.

This girl has the same uncombed hair Casey did, although her face is wider, her eyes less bright. I turn away, wishing I could see Casey one more time, just to be sure she's safe.

I throw my bowling ball with my left hand, since the right is still weak. As I watch the ball veer slightly off-center, I run my fingers over my stubbly hair—still engraved with the wing pattern—willing the ball's path straight.

I end up with only one pin standing.

"Imagine the last pin is Matt and then knock it down," Alena says. "He deserves to get clobbered."

Sal's bronze eyes find mine. I remember how I wanted to hammerfist Matt just like I did Neanderthal. I shudder.

Life is brutal. Horrible things happen to innocent people. But there's more than one way to punch back.

"Matt's already getting what he deserves." I take aim, thinking of Casey, and knock down the final pin.

ACKNOWLEDGMENTS

Although writing is a solitary job, a book is the combined effort of many people. Thanks to the Red Door Family Shelter in Toronto for the volunteer job at one of its facilities. Although the characters and situations in this book are a work of fiction, my experiences there helped make this story more authentic. Thanks to my early readers, who offered astute feedback on the work in progress: Pat Bourke, Anne Laurel Carter, Paige Krossing, Tess Krossing, Patricia McCowan, Mahtab Narsimhan, Cheryl Rainfield, Karen Rankin, Rilla Ross, Erin Thomas and Andrew Tolson. Thanks to Harry Endrulat of The Rights Factory and Sarah Harvey of Orca Book Publishers for believing in the manuscript, and thanks to the Orca team for helping to produce this book. Finally, thanks to my family, who supports my writing in so many ways.

KAREN KROSSING is addicted to stories. She began to create her own stories when she was eight, and today she writes novels and short stories for children and teens. Karen also encourages new writers through workshops for kids, teens and adults. Karen lives with her family in Toronto, Ontario. *Punch Like a Girl* is her seventh novel. For more information, visit karenkrossing.com.